# Faces in thé Sky

## BY IVEY WEAVER

Faces in the Sky by Ivey Weaver
Copyright © 2018 by Ivey Weaver
Cover by: Black Reign Graphics
Editor – Michael Ray King
218p. ill. cm.
ISBN  978-1-935795-52-0

LCCN 2018941608



Michael Ray King Publishing
PO Box 353431
Palm Coast, FL 32135-3431

Printed in the United States of America

# Acknowledgments

I would like to express my gratitude to all the people who were involved with this book and saw it through. To all those who know that I suffer from bipolar disorder and accept me for me, I thank you. It is my disorder that allows me to have the imagination that I do.

Words will never be able to properly express to you what you meant to me and how much you have impacted my life. To my wife who has been my anchor in life, I could not have done this book without your encouraging words and your unyielding belief that this is what I'm supposed to be doing.

You are my rock and you offered endless hours of support when I was going back and forth with the little details for *Faces in the Sky*. You became my biggest fan when I completed the book. Your dedication to make my dream of writing come true will forever remain in my heart and memory. I love you with every little piece of my existence.

Caleb, my son, you are one of the most important people in my life. Thank you for your love and belief in *Faces in the Sky*. Without you by my side, I wouldn't have been able to complete my book. You are so intelligent. A mother could not have picked a better son than you if she had the choice. I love you.

I express my ultimate thanks to my publisher Michael Ray King. Thank you for taking the chance to read my book. Thank you for agreeing to spend tedious hours editing my book. I am humbled by the way you have impacted my life. Your words continue to encourage me to write. You told me to write my truth and ever since that day I have been putting my pen to work! None of this would have been possible without you.

I would like to thank my Al, my oldest brother and best friend. You read my book and kept it real with me when I needed it the most. You continue to offer me substance when I feel lost and am in need of advice.

I cannot thank Black Reign Graphics enough for my excellent book cover.

Last, please forgive me for those who I have failed to mention by name. Please know that I will forever be humbled by having you in my life. To my friends who stayed patient and continue to stand by my side, I thank you.

# Dedication

To my loving wife Kyeesha Weaver and my son Caleb, which without them this work of fiction would not have been completed. Your undying support is the glue that holds me together. Your love is the motivation which allows me to continue to put pen to paper and tell a story.

To all those out there who are suffering with a mental illness or abuse, I dedicate *Faces in the Sky* to you. Please know that there are ways to become better. If it weren't for our experiences in life, there wouldn't be television or music. We as people must go through trials in life in order to learn and become better humans. Know that you are not alone.

# Table of Contents

Prologue


My life unfolds as an unpredictable twist and turn of events. The journey follows roads which lead to one place or another. Sometimes the way lies cluttered with debris crossing a certain path. You must choose another path. Then you stumble upon a crossroad and can't decide which way to go.

You take a chance. You choose the road you believe will lead you the right direction, only to find a dead end.

Stuck and confused, you don't give up because what good does that do? Once you decide to keep pushing forward you realize

there are way too many bumps in the pavement.
Some things in life come at you too hard. There
are so many different choices you must make
and many sacrifices to get to where you're
going.  Some of them good. Some not so much.
Close your eyes, take a deep breath and join me
on this journey through life's roller-coaster
ride.

## *Chapter one*

1985. That's when it all started when my mother discovered she was pregnant.

I was born at Fish Memorial Hospital in Deland, Florida. My mother, Margaret Flowers, would tell me about my birth as a bed time story. She would say I was her "little miracle" baby because doctors said she was unable to have children. When my mother found she was pregnant, she stopped drinking.

Apparently, I was eager to come out because I entered the world two months early. My mother always said, "God has a specific purpose for you and you are destined to do great things." Upon my arrival, I cried and was handed over to a woman who would become my first best friend.

By the time I was 5 years old I discovered the meaning of loss. My Grandmother, who was like a second mother to me, passed away. She had been ill and couldn't hold on any longer. I remember vivid things about that day. People say I was too young to remember. Images scroll through my head of being picked up in a long black car and taken to a church.

I recall climbing out of this car. I looked up at a hill of stairs that led to giant red doors. Everyone climbing these stairs were escorted by older men and women wearing dark suits with gloves. Sadness came over me in waves like an ocean crashing on the shore.

I smell despair in the air. At the time, I don't know about death or how to respond. I do the first thing that comes natural to me – I cry. I don't know why I'm crying.

I glance at my mother. I see a river of tears streaming down her cheeks. The tear drops remind me of rain but for some reason they were falling from her face instead of the sky. She holds my hand in hers; she walks us to the front row and sits me next to my aunt. After a few moments, she lets go of my hand as she continues to talk to the people standing around her.

I feel alone and turn to my aunt for comfort. She wraps her arms around me and tries to console me but it isn't enough. As any five-year-old would do feeling alone, I cry. My crying must have grabbed my mother's attention because I find myself safe again in her arms.

Sitting in my mother's lap, I listen to people talk, sing, and cry.  After an eternity, she takes my hand and leads me to what looks like a giant wooden box. As we approach the box, I notice her grip gets tighter and this startles me.

Now curious as to what lies in this box, I reach my arms up to her. She turns and picks me up, lifting me high enough to peer down and see my grandmother lying there as if she were asleep. *It must be a bed for adults* I say to myself.

Although she looks peaceful, her body is motionless as though she is in the best sleep in the world. I'm confused and wonder why she is lying in a box and not in her bed at home.

Again, the feeling of sadness envelopes me and I cry. My mother tries to soothe me but it doesn't help. She squeezes me tighter in her arms and we walk away. I stare over her shoulder seizing what I didn't realize would be my last sight of her.

I begin to wonder why my mother doesn't just reach over and wake her up so she may go home with us. Why are we leaving her here? Back in the limousine, everyone remains quiet.

That is all I remember from that day. As I got older I realized my grandmother had died and what I witnessed was a familiar scene when someone died. Still, at the age of 31, not a day goes by that my grandmother's death doesn't bother me. I continue to miss her and get very sad when I think about her.

As an adult, I often visit her gravesite. As I do this day, I attempt to talk to her but the words won't come out. I'm lost as to what I should or shouldn't say to her. I don't even know where to start.

Instead, my anger gets the best of me and I scream out. I know she's not there to comfort me. I become very emotional and cry for her to return to me. I struggle to think about the good memories that will be with me forever.

One of those memories I am fond of takes place at age three. My father was working on my grandmother's house. He was fixing the roof and was using tar to do so. Me being the explorer I am, I went to check out this pond of black stuff in this big white bucket.

I stood on my tip toes and leaned over to peer into the bucket. I obviously got too close and toppled over head first.

I chuckle at the thought and remember hearing my grandmother's screeching voice from in the house. Next thing I remember, she ran outside and scooped me up, took me into the house and placed me in the sink. She talked gibberish to herself while she cleaned me up. All the while, I'm startled by the warm and gooey tar.

Wiping tears from my eyes, I gaze at my grandmother's tombstone. Again, I am at a loss for words. What do I say to the woman who was more than a mother to me? How do I begin to tell her how much her death haunts me? How do I tell her how angry I am at her for leaving me alone?

I bolt upright and furiously wipe tears
from my face. I turn and leave.  I stroll
away from her tombstone much like I
walked away from her lying in that wooden
box. I would face life's harsh realities alone
and afraid.

## *Chapter 2*


I tap my fingers on the bar. I signal for another.

I'm at my second home, The Watering Hole. I perch on my usual stoop. Lifting my glass, I swallow my problems. Just like my struggles burn me in real life, I feel them burn my throat. I close my eyes and wait for the burn to pass. Drinking has become my new medicine to drown out the taunting voices and the haunting pain.

I drink until I'm numb. Eventually the voices fade away. Void of emotion I get lost in the bliss of nothingness. Sky Flowers, that's my name. Standing at 5'7" my lanky form fits my small bone structure. Sharp angles define my face and leave me with an androgynous look.

Most times I'm either referred to as ma'am or sir but it doesn't bother me. Being a lesbian has taught me to not be sensitive to other people's words.

The color of the whisky I'm drinking matches my dark features. I have long black lashes and deep brown eyes. I am accustomed to being referred to as good looking but I pay little or no attention to this detail.

Gulping down another drink, I feel that familiar tingle and embrace it. The whiskey loosens me up making my limbs feel mushy. When I sit in the bar I rarely look up or pay attention to anything going on around me. People come and go.

To be honest, I couldn't care less about anyone or anything while I'm here. People drink for their own reasons. Some of their reasons may be good while others are bad. I barely notice when someone takes the stool next to mine. I signal for another drink.

"That bad, huh?"

I chuckle and don't look up. I nod my head hoping that the person speaking takes it as a sign I would rather not be bothered. Instead the voice continues. Rolling my eyes, I look up at the voice.

To say the woman was gorgeous would not do her justice. She owns a set of full red lips and sultry blue eyes in which I would love to drown.

Staring into her eyes reminds me of swimming in the ocean. I desire to dive into them. I inspect her body with a slow scan from head to toe and back. I am pleased at how sexy this woman is. She sports nicely tanned skin and her cleavage is definitely inviting. I work not to drool thinking about the things I could do with them.

I clear my throat and realize she has caught me staring. She glances at me with a peculiar face. I drag my eyes back up her body and haven't the faintest clue as to what she has said.

"I'm sorry, what did you say?"

Chuckling she says, "Do you come here often?"

Shaking my head I say "Yes. I know the owners."

"Oh, I just moved here and was curious about the scenery."

"Oh yeah? Where did you move from?"

Again, I rake my eyes over her body. I notice she's wearing a pale grey skirt that has risen up from sitting on the bar stool. Her legs run long and her skin appears supple and soft. My hands itch to be on her.

"Boston," she responds.

I laugh. "What brings you to this dark place?"

"A fresh start."

Her answers are vague. I don't push for more. Honestly, all I'm thinking is that I want two things. A couple more drinks and to take this beautiful woman to bed. "Sounds like a good enough reason I suppose."

I shrug and signal the bartender for another. "Would you like a drink?"

"Thanks. A strawberry daiquiri."

I just nod my head and gulp down my drink. I lean close to her. "You're gorgeous."

She blushes. "Casey-."

"Huh?"

"My name."

"Oh! Sky," I say in a voice that sounds uninterested.

"So, how long have you lived here?" Casey asks.

"A while," I state, not really eager to explain. Luckily, she doesn't continue this line of questioning. Casey reaches over and takes my hand.  She pulls me away from the bar.

Confused, I follow. She wraps her arms around my shoulders and sways her hips to the beat of the music in front of me. I wrap my arms around her waist and let her lead me into joining her rhythm.

I don't feel like dancing but I can put up with it - if it gets me laid. Laughing and shaking my head, I wonder when I became so pitiful. I close my eyes allowing my ears take in the melodic woman singing about her heart being broken.  The song takes me to another place.

*I was nine years old. My aunt and her two weird sons were staying with my mom and me. It was the first time I experienced hurt at the hands of a family member.*

*Chris and Jason were older than me by what seemed like a lot of years. We still hung out though. They would do things like torture and hang animals on crosses. Although they were weird, I thought they were cool because they were older than me.*

*I followed them around. I didn't care for animals much, so I thought - whatever. One day we were out exploring the woods looking for small unsuspecting animals, when Jason came over to me and asked if I had a boyfriend.*

*"No! Gross!" I wasn't interested in boys and I knew deep inside I never would. I felt I was different and it scared me. I remember hearing people talk about how disgusting it was to be gay and it made me feel lonely and different.*

*Was that what I was? I didn't know. I was too young to even begin to tackle that question. I just knew I felt different.*

*"Why do you think that's gross?"*

*Shrugging my shoulders, I didn't want to seem childish. I quickly thought of a response.*

*"I haven't found the right boy yet. As the words spilled out of my mouth, I cringed but hearing those words in my mind, I thought I appeared mature. Happy with myself, I smile and continue to follow him through the woods.*

*Later that night back at home, I get a shower and prepare myself for bed. I kiss my mother and climb into bed. Not sleepy, I lay there thinking about our stroll through the woods. My thoughts are interrupted by a soft knock at the door.  I get up and open it, to find Jason standing there towering over me.*

*"Hey," he says in a soft voice.*

*"Hi," I say with an inquiring tone.*

*"Come to my room for a second."*

*"Okay." I follow my cousin to his room thinking he's going to show me something cool. We sit on the bed and he says.*

*"Remember what I asked you earlier?"*

*"Yeah,"*

*"What if I'm the right boy for you?"*

*Scrunching my eyebrows together with a slight snicker I say, "You can't be because you're my cousin silly."*

*"Yes I can."*

*Nervously, I pretend to yawn. I tell him, "I'm going back to bed. That long walk today made me tired."*

*He places his large hairy hand on my shoulder and says, "I'm not finished talking to you."*

*Panic sets in. My heart races. The pounding in my chest echoes in my head. He leans in. He kisses me sloppily. I push him away. This only serves to encourage him. He touches my body. All over. I taste fear.*

*"No!" I say in my loudest voice without screaming.*

*He shoves my face into the mattress. "Shut up before I hurt you."*

*I bite my lip. I stay quiet. Afraid of what he might do to me, I lay there shocked at what is happening. He pulls the shorts of my pajamas off. I bury my face deeper into the mattress trying to escape this nightmare.*

*I hear what sounds like him undressing. His private part touches mine. It feels disgusting. Tears stream my cheeks creating a soaked spot on the sheets.*

*I lay paralyzed, not knowing what to do. I try to make my mind escape my body. I must have blacked out at some point.*

*When I came to, he was pulling my shorts and underwear back up my legs. He sent me back to my room.*

*I curl up into a ball and cry into my pillow. The next day I decide I don't want to play with them and pretend to be sick. I stay in bed and think about what has happened.*

*I finally get up because I don't want my mom to notice anything. I bathe. I begin scrubbing at my skin furiously hoping to erase last night.*

*No matter how much I scrub, I still feel dirty. Bile rises up in my throat. I run over to the toilet emptying out my stomach. Shakily, I stand and dry off. I dress quickly and go back to my room.*

*Again, that night he knocks at my door. Scared, I act like I'm asleep. The ploy doesn't work. He barges into my room again and drags me by the hand to his room.*

*"You better not say a word about this or I'll hurt you."*

*I nod my head yes unable to find my voice. My throat feels dry and my voice feels trapped like I have ran through the desert and there is no liquid in it. He shoves me on the bed roughly and undresses us both.*

*Closing my eyes, I tell my mind to drift to somewhere else – anywhere else but here. So, as my mind follows my direction, it drifts, not exactly sure where but I know it's better than where I am at this moment. I pray this ends soon. It does.*

*Back in my room I bite into my pillow and scream. I wonder why this is happening to me. I think about how I'm going to stop it from happening again. I turn over in my bed, fold my hands and pray to God that Jason stops hurting me.*

*My prayers go unanswered. For several months he continues his routine of waking me and dragging me to his room. My body follows his commands in fear that if I fight back, he will hurt me even more.*

*When I'm alone in my room, I think to myself - fight him! But when the time comes and he herds me to his room, I think – what's the point? He's bigger and stronger than me. I can't do anything to stop it.*

*To be honest, I stop caring. I feel like I must have done something wrong to deserve this and God is punishing me. Lying on the bed, my soul goes to a place where it's dark. I go numb.*

*I lay there and wait for him to finish. He pushes me away signaling me he's done and I fumble trying to pull my clothes up. My mother bursts through the door. Frozen, I just stand there. Scared I drop my head and stare at the floor.*

*"What the hell is going on?" she screams. Shocked and afraid, I just stand*

*there. She walks over and grabs my hand and pulls me out of the room.*

*Not saying a word, she kneels in front of me and looks at me without making eye contact. I begin to cry hysterically.*

Shaking the memory from my mind, I break away from Casey's embrace and go over to the bar where my drink is waiting. Gulping it down, I toss some money on the counter.

"Do you want to get out of here?"

Casey cocks her head to the side and nods in agreement. I grab her hand and I pull her through the door.

"Your place," I say, not really asking.

"Ok."

I kiss her lips and watch as she strides to her car. Casey has a black Mercedes with tinted windows. Her car matches her sophistication and doesn't surprise me. I drive behind her in my red Camaro.

# Chapter 3

All sorts of things run through my mind. As I focus on her black Mercedes I'm reminded of Sharon.

*I had turned 18 and had the first flight out of the hell-hole I called home. I had met this woman online and she promised me a different scene. For my birthday, she promised to buy me a ticket to come see her.*

*I thought, "What the hell." Walking through the airport, I was mesmerized by all the people rushing around like worker ants, hurrying towards their destination.*

*My gaze was interrupted when I felt someone brush past me.  I notice a woman and her crying baby in a hurry running past. Shaking my head I look around and see a line where people were anxiously waiting to get their tickets.*

*I take a deep breath and pull my suitcase behind me. I stumble clumsily in that direction. Up at the counter a woman rolls her eyes and says, "How may I help you?"*

*In my mind I think she doesn't really mean this but oh well. I clear my throat and say, "I guess I need to get my ticket that was purchased for me."*

*"Ok – ID please."*

*I dig through my pockets, pull out my ID and hand it to her. She mumbles incoherently under her breath and begins typing. Finally she hands me my ID back and I wait.*

*Moments later I am handed my ticket to freedom. Smiling, I thank the lady and head off in the direction where my future awaits me. My nerves start to get the best of me and my breathing increases as I sit on the plane. I ball my fists and reach for my phone and headphones.*

*I place them on my ears, lean back and close my eyes. Hearing the music, my nerves settle and my heart beat returns to normal. Caught off guard, I jump to someone tapping me on the shoulder.*

*I remove my ear buds and glance up to see a man standing over me. He is a little on the heavy side and wears a sweat-soaked graphic tee-shirt. His large nose and eyes fit his huge head.*

*I attempt not to stare. I notice his faded grey sweat pants and tee shirt has remnants of a superhero on it that looks as if it has seen the washer too many times. I cringe hoping he's at the wrong seat.*

*"I have the window seat, however, I'd rather not squeeze through. Do you mind?"*

*"No, it's cool," I mumble, thinking, "thank God I didn't have to meet his sweat soaked clothes up close and personal." I move closer to the window, pop my earbuds back into my ears, and turn to the window. As I gaze out the window I see all sorts of people on the ground readying the plane.*

*I am fascinated by the way they move. Their movements appear choreographed as they move in sync with one another getting their jobs done. Scanning over the people, I concentrate on the runway and I am mesmerized at the things that we have on earth. Planes fly out every day, all day, taking people from one place to another.*

*I glance to my left. I see a plane come into sight getting ready to take off. It reminds me of a large bird as it propels itself up the runway. The aircraft glides, picking up speed until at once it is lifted off the ground.*

*My head is smashed against the window as I strain to see how the plane moves. The plane continues to go until I have to squint to see it. When the plane disappears, I settle back in my seat and wait.*

*Two women come out looking like twins and begin instructing passengers to turn off*

*all mobile and electronic devices until
prompted to turn them back on. I roll my
eyes as I turn my phone onto airplane mode
and look up.*

*"Ladies and gentlemen, the Captain has
turned on the Fasten Seat Belt sign. If you
haven't already done so, please stow your
carry-on luggage underneath the seat in
front of you or in an overhead bin. Please
take your seat and fasten your seat belt.
And also make sure your seat back and
folding trays are in their full upright
position.*

*If you are seated next to an emergency
exit, please read carefully the special
instructions card located by your seat. If
you do not wish to perform the functions
described in the event of an emergency,
please ask a flight attendant to reseat you.*

*We remind you that this is a non-smoking flight. Smoking is prohibited on the entire aircraft, including the lavatories. Tampering with, disabling or destroying the lavatory smoke detectors is prohibited by law. If you have any questions about our flight today, please don't hesitate to ask one of our flight attendants. Thank you."*

*My nerves flutter again as I feel the engine come to life. I draw in a deep breath. I swallow multiple times as I work to shake off this scary feeling. The plane moves up the runway. I grip my seat until my knuckles turn white. I'm hoping that everything goes as planned.*

*As the plane speeds up, I feel it bounce up and down. After closing my eyes as tight as I can, we are in the air and off to Ohio. Arriving at my destination, I scan the crowd for a familiar face. Looking through thousands of people I feel my anxiety and nervousness return.*

*I pull my suitcase out of the way of people rushing around me, I spot a woman that seems familiar. She smiles in my direction and waves me over. Disappointed, I think to myself from a distance that she doesn't really look like the picture she sent me. As I get closer, I take in her looks.*

*Her hair falls from the top of her head light brown, wavy, and curly. Her face is round with small eyes and a button nose. She is plump but not overly so. I scan her body and notice that there really isn't anything special about her to catch my attention. She is average height with average looks. Thinking it could be worse, I continue to walk over to her.*

*Once I reach her, we awkwardly hug and she tells me how excited she is that I'm here. I look at her and once I hear her voice I am reminded of a familiar person.*

*This is the woman on the other end of the phone I have been communicating with for the past couple of years. We head out the door and I take in my surroundings. Trees and tall buildings tower over me everywhere. I breathe in the fresh air. The day is a little chilly and slightly windy but a welcome change from the hot weather in Florida.*

*"How was your flight?"*

*"It was good," I say.*

*Nodding, she smiles at me and I'm struck by how beautiful it makes her look. Again, I think it could be worse and tell myself to make the best of things.*

*"Are you hungry?"*

*"I could eat." Just then my stomach rumbles loudly and I clear my throat, embarrassed.*

*"I'll take that as a yes," she says.*

*We get to her car and it's a white Mercedes. I smile. I pick my bag up and carefully place it in the trunk. I walk around to the passenger side and get in the car.*

*Once inside I put on my seatbelt. She glances over at me and smiles and fires the engine. She places her hand on the steering wheel and pulls out into traffic. The buildings seem so tall, like giants, as if they could reach the sky. I am amazed at how big things seem. Nothing at all like what I'm used to. Lost in thought I feel her eyes on me.*

*"Are you glad to be here?" she asks.*

*"Yes. Just tired."*

*But that was only half the truth. I was a little nervous and didn't know what to expect. Hell I didn't even know what she wanted from me. Did she think we were in a relationship? Was she looking to get married?*

*Oh gosh, what have I gotten into? All these questions kept spinning around and around in my head. Mentally telling my mind to shut up, I try to start a conversation.*

*"So is your house around here?"*

*"Yes. Not that far from here actually."*

*"Cool," I say and mentally cringe at how childish I must appear. Come on. Get it together. This woman is accomplished and*

*older. Pull it together.  Laughing to myself,
I think, "well I'm only 18 and she's 41.
What do you expect?" Shaking my head, I
once again tell my mind to shut up.*

*"How was your birthday?"*

*"It was good I guess."*

*"What did you do?"*

*"Nothing much. The usual. Oh, my
friends took me to a club for the first time."*

*"Oh, you didn't tell me that."*

*"It was a last minute thing".*

*She becomes quiet and I wonder if I
should have said anything at all about the
club as it seems to have upset her. I sit
quietly and wonder why the mood has
changed.*

*Finally we pull into a McDonald's. I take off my seatbelt and get out of the car. Walking around the car I open Sharon's door.*

*"Thank you," she smiles.*

*I nod. She clutches my hand and we start to walk inside. Butterflies form in my stomach. Smiling inside, I hold the door for her to walk through. We order our food and take a seat. Munching on fries, I thank her for the meal.*

*"You're welcome baby." She stares at me and butterflies circle my stomach. "I want to kiss you," she says.*

*"I do too."*

*"Well when we get to the house we can get a little more comfortable."*

*"Ok," I mumble. I start to wonder what she means by getting a little more comfortable. Does she mean sex? How is it going to be with her? All of these things are going through my head and I don't realize that she has already thrown away our trash.*

*"Ready?"*

*"Yes." Standing up and stretching, I feel myself becoming tired. Back in the car she turns on some soft music and I relax and lean against the door.*

*"Hey," she whispers, gently shaking my shoulder.*

*"Mmm," I moan. I must have drifted off to sleep because now we're in front of what must be her house. It's gorgeous and immense.*

*I clear my throat and stutter, "You live here?"*

*Chuckling she nods yes and happily snaps, "Let's go."*

*I get out of the car and look around. The neighborhood appears quiet as if no one even lives here. The only sounds are birds chirping in the distance. Glancing again at her house, I see that it's a sort of charcoal gray and black.*

*It's a massive two story brick home with vines growing on the front of it. It reminds me of a house you would see in the movies. I can't wait to get inside and see what it looks like.*

*I draw a breath and gather my things I follow her inside. Once inside the house, my breath is taken away at how gorgeous everything looks. The walls are different colors lined with huge paintings. The*

*kitchen is the size of my house and I wonder
how much money she has.*

*"Come, I'll show you your room." I
follow her down a hall and to the right. She
opens the door and it's spacious. The bed
looks three times the size of my old bed. It is
made up with black and red sheets. The
walls are also red with silver circles
painted on them. I walk over to the bed and
notice the closet is just as big.*

*Geez, I could just sleep in there I think.
Shaking my head I turn to tell her how
much I appreciate this. She puts her hand
up and silences me.*

*"No need, I'm happy you're finally
here."*

*I walk over to her and with my best
confidence I kiss her lips. It's a shy kiss at
first. She instantly deepens the kiss and runs*

*her hands up and down my arms. I grab her waist and pull her closer to me.*

*"Mmm," she moans.*

*I push her towards the bed. I remove her shirt. This part I can do. I'm good at all things sex. I've known that about myself for a long time. Our kisses become furious as we undress each other. The butterflies in my stomach reach a new height. I tell myself to calm down.*

*I leave her mouth and trail kisses all along her neck. She moans, so I continue to explore. I leave her soft skin long enough to remove her shirt and bra.*

*Her breasts are full with dark nipples. I lower my head and take her left nipple into my mouth. Again she moans and pushes my head deeper, encouraging me to suck harder.*

*I take her hint and begin to nibble her nipple. Not wanting the other one to become jealous, I repeat the same action on her right breast. She falls back onto the bed and pulls me on top of her. I start grinding my pelvis into hers.*

*"Please get my clothes off, I want to feel you!"*

*I slide down her body and unbutton her pants. I yank them down her legs along with her underwear impatiently. I pull off my clothes in a hurry. Settling back on top of her, I kiss her lips again. We both moan at the feeling of our skin touching.*

*"I've waited so long for this. I have wanted you for so long and you are finally here."*

*Staring down at her I become lost in her eyes. "Me too I say," truly meaning it. I* slide my knee in between her legs. I feel her wetness.

"Do you feel it?" she asks.

"Yes."

"That's what you do to me."

My ego the size of a football field, I make it my mission to please her. I replace my knee with my fingers. She feels warm and soft. My hand glides through her wetness and she cries out her pleasure. "I can't hold it."

"Don't," I whisper. Not allowing her to come down from her first orgasm. I quickly slide my fingers inside of her.

I hear someone clear their throat in the distance and my body stills.

"What the..." My words are cut off by her gasping.

*"Peter, this isn't what it looks like!"*

*Peter? I ask in my head.*

*"Oh no." The man stares at us with his dark eyes. Frantically I pull at my clothes and sit up, thinking, what was the point of trying to cover up. I run into the bathroom. I slam and lock the door. Sinking to the floor I grab my head.*

*What the fuck is this about? Is he an ex or something? I thought she was gay. Oh God, is this a threesome? Shaking my head I hurry and get dressed. As I'm getting myself together, I hear muffled voices on the other side of the door.  I push my ear into the door as best I can, straining to make sense of the mumble.*

*"I go out every day and work hard so that you can fuck around?"*

*"No honey," she cries.*

*"Obviously this was no accident," the man yells. "I told you to have your gay flings somewhere else. Not in our home!"*

*"I'm sorry."*

Cringing at the memory, I follow Casey into a parking lot filled with cars. *This must be where she lives*, I think to myself. The apartment complex looks recently built. The buildings are all different colors. I think the same builder must have done every apartment complex in Florida. Getting out of my car, she struts over to me.

"Hey, follow me," she says.

I take Casey's hand and together we walk towards the elevator. Locked in on her hips swaying, my palms tingle to touch more of her.

I pull her back against me. We come to a complete stop as I crush our lips together.

I kiss her hard and run my tongue against her mouth. Opening, she allows my tongue inside. We move towards the elevator at a very slow pace. I use my time wisely, and run my hands all over her body. Casey moans.

"Slow down baby let me get the door open," Casey says breathless.

I chuckle and release my hold on her. We finally manage to part and get on the elevator without any further delays. Arriving at her apartment door my body tingles to get next to hers. As soon as she unlocks the door, she pulls me through it laughing.

I back her up against the door and resume my kisses. I run my hands up to Casey's hair and set it free. I run my hands through her long strands taking in its softness.

"Damn," I grumble as she rakes her nails up my stomach catching me off guard. I want to touch her everywhere at once. My confidence kicks up a notch as I make her moan again. My need for control is sometimes startling to me. Taking her shirt into my hands I pull it up and off her body.

It's dark in her apartment with only a beam of florescent light peering in from the parking lot, just the way I like it. Darkness matches my mood. I release her breasts and watch with fascination as they sway from being set free. Taking each one into my hands I become lost.

I lower my face from hers and take one then the other into my mouth. *Better than I expected*, I think. She moans and tells me to take her to bed.

With her leading the way we stumble into her bedroom. I'm too preoccupied with taking her clothes off to look around. After I get her naked, I let her watch me get undressed. Her eyebrows rise as I lift my shirt over my head.

I'm not wearing a bra so I stand there in my nakedness. Casey licks her lips in approval and I take that as my cue to continue.

I slowly unbutton my pants and let them fall to the floor. Standing in only my boy shorts, I move towards her again. I push her further up onto the bed. I remove the last barrier between us. Admiring her beauty I get lost staring at her. She completely takes my breath away.

I resume my earlier actions. Her breasts rest in my hands again. I tug at her nipples as I fall to my knees. Sensing what I'm about to do, Casey spreads her legs and shows me what I've been dying to see.

I grin and lean forward to blow on her exposed skin. This gets the desired effect because she spreads her legs further apart. Licking her belly button she begins to chuckle.

"Someone's ticklish," I say in an amused tone.

I continue my journey downward. I lick and kiss her inner thighs. I take my time enjoying every inch of her soft skin. This is something that mustn't be rushed. This woman needs to be worshipped and I plan on doing so. Impatiently, she places her hands in my hair encouraging me to give her what she wants.

"Patience," I whisper.

Lifting her leg over my shoulder I breathe in her scent. It smells fresh like a beautiful red rose blooming in spring. Leaning in, I hesitate to taste her. I want this moment to become ingrained in my memory. Finally, I lean in and taste Casey.

"God yes," she moans.

Stunned at how wonderful she tastes, I dive in. Sucking on her lips I try to get more nectar to come out for me. She thrusts her hips into my face and I become lost in what I'm doing.

Her moans encourage me to ravish her more. After a couple of sucks and licks, I feel her tense all over. I speed up my tongue until at last she spills out.

"Fuck, you're amazing," Casey says gasping for air.

I drink in the sight of her, taken back by her beauty. "I'm just getting started," I growl as I dive back into our passion.

After what seems like hours Casey lays spent and sated. I ease out of her embrace, taking care not to wake her, I slide out of bed and quickly get dressed. One last gaze at her beautiful body, I turn, sprint to the door and leave.

# Chapter 4

Cool night air jostles my brain full of thoughts. I don't really think about the stranger laying upstairs. She is just another escape for me. An outlet. All of them are the same. This is what my life has become. A never ending tangle of bodies and sex.

I tap my pockets and finally feel my cigarettes. I lean against my car, light one up, and inhale. I close my eyes and blow the smoke out of my mouth hoping that it will erase tonight's event. After a few drags, I flick the butt into the shadows. I briefly think I need to quit but what the hell.

In my car, I whiz in and out of the little traffic on the road back to my home. My doom.

Once there and inside, I walk through my dark apartment not needing to turn on any lights. I know this place inside and out. I have lived here for the past six years. I could walk it with my eyes closed. I take out a beer from the fridge, pop the top and gulp down half of it.

Grabbing another one, I flop onto the leather sofa. I finish my beer and take out my phone. I have several missed calls. "Nick, geez. How many times did you need to call?"

I squint to see that it's well past four in the morning. I send my best friend a text letting her know I'm safe. I throw my phone down and close my eyes. My breathing slows as I instantly drift off to sleep.

BANG! BANG! BANG!

"What the hell!" I bolt upright and instantly regret the fast movement. My head spins and feels as though a knife has been pushed through it. I close my eyes and work to control my breathing.

BANG! BANG! BANG!

"Come on Sky open the door!" Nick yells.

I struggle to push the words out of my mouth and attempt to yell, "I'm coming!" but my throat is so dry the words come out as a mere whisper. Barely able to stand, I stumble over my shoes cursing as I hit my toe on the table. I make my way to the door. I yank the door open and stare at Nick with a death glare.

"Well you had a long night I see."

I stagger back to the sofa, grumble, and sit. I hold my head in my hands.

"That bad?" Nick asks.

"Something like that," I mumble. "Pills?" I plead.

Nick gets up and goes to the kitchen. She returns with Tylenol and a glass of water. *God bless her* I think to myself. I swallow the pills and the water, choke, and begin to cough. Nick pats my back and I instantly calm.

"You're killing yourself," Nick states, sounding genuinely worried.

"Please not now," I plead holding up my hand.

"What's her name?" Nick asks in a questioning tone.

"Who?" I say confused.

"From last night. What's her name?"

"Casey, but what does it matter?"

"I don't know, you just seem bothered. Did something else happen last night?" Nick asks in a curious tone.

"Pssshhh, I left just like I always do," I say, feeling anger rise inside of me.

"You're right, that's what you do," Nick says.

Irritated and not wanting to talk anymore, I storm into the bathroom and slam the door.

Nicolette, a.k.a Nick, has been my friend for as long as I can remember. No matter where I moved, we always found each other. Nick became the only constant in my ever changing world. The only person I could trust. At some point we tried having a relationship but fast realized we were better as friends.

Nick is about the same height as me with short brown hair. She's not overly girly but not too boyish either. She pulls off the in-between really well. She has dark eyes and tanned skin. Nick has a natural beauty about her that makes her seem confident. In the bathroom I look at myself in the mirror while the water heats up for my shower.

As the mirror fogs from the steam, it causes my reflection to fade and become distorted. I mull over Nick's comments about my usual behavior of leaving without saying goodbye. This causes me to reflect on the person I have become.

What's happened to me? Do I really care that a woman wakes up feeling some type of way because I left without a word? I shake my head. I say no to myself and shrug at even letting the thought cross mind.

I don't care. It's better that I leave Casey before she leaves me. People always end up leaving eventually. I learned that lesson early on in life.

*I was 13. My parents were having another one of their great arguments. I slam my bedroom door and pull the covers over my head. "Not again," I say. I can hear my mother yelling about this and that and my father is sitting there like usual not saying much.*

*Sometimes I think he must be afraid of my mother because she hits him and throws things and he never does anything about it.*

*I place my headphones on, and turn up the volume as loud as it can go. I drown out their voices. I replace racket, with Birdy singing about 'Beautiful Lies.' Her voice soothes me as I sink lower into my bed hoping the night comes to an end quickly.*

*Restless and failing at falling asleep, I notice the house is finally quiet. I snuggle under my covers, curl up, and fall asleep. When I wake up, I go through the boring routines of the morning.*

*After finishing in the bathroom I wander into the living room. My mother lies on the sofa with a tear stained face. I gently walk over to her and sit down.*

*"Mom?" I whisper.*

*She doesn't respond but gathers me up into her arms. I hug her back.*

*She clears her throat and says, "I need you to listen to me."*

*I look at her with questions rifling through my eyes.*

*"Your father," her voice cracks as she tries to hold her tears in. She clears her throat and tries again. "He's gone."*

*She falls apart in my arms and I hold onto her for dear life. I clutch her even tighter to comfort her. I don't even notice the tears that run down my own face. I think to myself, he didn't even say goodbye.*

I run my hands over my face, pick up my toothbrush and begin to brush my teeth. After I rinse my mouth clean, I turn and get in the shower. The shower helps me feel like a brand new person. I follow the smells of food into the kitchen where Nick has set my plate. I sit and beckon her to join me. She sits and we eat in silence. I can feel the wheels turning in her head.

"Please don't start on your tangent again," I plead.

"I'm just worried about you."

"I can take care of myself," I say a little harsher than I intend. Noticeably hurt by my words, I try to apologize. "I'm sorry…I -" She shrugs my apology off and stands up.

"Well I have to go, I'm going to be late for work."

I shake my head and realize I'm an asshole. I am lost as to what to do.

"Ok," I whisper feeling defeated.

I walk her to the door. She kisses my cheek and leaves. Closing the door I rest my head against it. *Way to go asshole* my mind chimes.

# *Chapter 5*

I once again sit alone at the bar drowning my sorrows.

"Another," I say loudly. The bartender saunters over and places another drink in front of me. "What's up sexy?" she says.

"Nothing. Same ol' bullshit different day," I reply. Stacy is the owner of the bar. We ended up sleeping together one drunken night before her and Nick hooked up. I laugh at the memory of the experience. It all seems so long ago.

"Pretty lady you went home with last night?" she asks inquisitively.

"Right," is all I reply. I don't share anymore details. She sounds like she is fishing for details just as Nick tried earlier.

Pouting she whines and says, "And?"

"And nothing," I say in a tone that means I'm serious.

"Geez who pissed in your cornflakes?" she says.

Shaking my head I say, "Why don't you do your job and get me another drink?"

Stacy grins. She knows I'm joking and walks away to get another drink. I watch her ass as she walks away from me. She glances back over her shoulder at me and smiles. "You know you want this," she purrs.

I don't answer as my phone chimes – text message. I quickly respond 'yes' to Valerie's request to me coming over to her place. Valerie is a woman that I hook up with on occasion. She is married and continues to step out on her husband.

Who am I to stop her? It works for me. I don't have to worry about her wanting to get serious. She stays busy with her husband so I don't have to see her all the time. I down my drink, throw money on the bar, and prepare to make my exit.

I'm not paying attention to where I'm walking and collide with another body. Grabbing onto the body, I steady myself and the other person. I'm about to apologize when I lock eyes with the last person I wanted to run into.

"Well we meet again," Casey says.

I don't reply but shake my head 'yes.' Her cheeks blush.

"I was just leaving," I say as I clear my throat.

To escape her presence before she can ask why I snuck out in the middle of the night, I skip past her without another glance.

Weeks pass turning into months without another Casey run-in. I continue on the path that I am familiar with. Drinking and hooking up with nameless women. Nick isn't at all pleased with my behavior and we have become distant.

I am a grown woman and in control of things. Most importantly in control of my life. Sipping my drink I look up and see a couple of younger girls whispering and pointing at me.

Cocking a brow, I continue to look at them. *Newbies* I say in my head. One of the girls strolls in my direction. I hold her gaze and can feel her nervous energy.

"Hi," she says.

"Hello."

"So my friends are here and we were wondering if you would like to join us?"

Pondering her question, I say, "No."

She looks defeated and I feel a little bad for her. She turns to walk away.

"You girls are free to join me though," I call out.

She smiles and says ok like three times. She hurries over to her friends and they all come to where I'm seated at the bar. There are three of them and they all look the same. Stacy cuts me a look and shakes her head. I stick my tongue out at her as she places a drink in front of me.

"Real mature," she whispers and walks away laughing. I give her the middle finger.

"So what's your names?" I ask, not really interested. The girl that walked over to me introduces herself as Deanna. Pointing to the others she introduces them as Drew and Laura.

"My name is Sky," I respond back.

Deanna settles in next to me and we all order a round of shots. "One. Two. Three. Chug!" We all down our drinks. I hear a couple of them cough. Laughing in my head, I think, *light weights*.

"Again!" I say.

Four shots later they are laughing at stuff I'm telling them and cheering me on.

I'm actually enjoying myself. I can't remember the last time I felt this free.

My hair is a curly mess all over my head. My shirt is unbuttoned and falling off my shoulders. I don't pay attention to this at all. I'm actually having fun.

Deanna and I down another shot. I hear her friends chanting "kiss – kiss-kiss." I turn to Deanna and pull her close. She looks nervous but I pull her to me anyway.

I touch my lips with hers and they're soft and inviting. Her friends cheer me on as I deepen the kiss. I stick my tongue in her mouth and suck on her bottom lip. We end the kiss soundly and she looks breathless and beautiful.

Her green eyes are glazed over and her cheeks red. Smiling, she throws her arms in the air and begins to cheer. I'm guessing it's her first kiss and I hope it was good for her.

Stacy loudly clears her throat and I turn to where she is directing her eyes. There stands the one person that I've been running from, glaring at me.

Caught up in all the excitement, I didn't notice Casey managed to quietly perch herself one seat over from me.

"Is there anyone in this town you haven't slept with?"

I shrug and say "yeah – these girls."

Not amused, she throws her drink in my face. I wipe my eyes. By the time I can see again, Casey is gone. Stacy walks over and hands me a towel.

"Needed to be cooled off I see?"

"Ha-ha," I say in an irritated voice.

I look over and see Deanna and her friends staring at me, shocked at Casey's antics. "That went well," I say nervously.

I take out a cigarette and light up. I give Stacy money for my drinks. "I'm going to call it a night." I get up, slap Deanna on the butt and walk out. I throw a goodbye over my shoulder.

Outside the air is stuffy. Humid. I look to see if Casey is anywhere in sight. Not seeing her, I walk quickly to my car, get in, and drive home. At home I turn the shower on and struggle to rid myself of the image of Casey's eyes glaring at me.

Why do I even care what she thinks? It's not like we are dating or anything. Geez she's immature for throwing her drink in my face. I guess I could have handled the situation better.

Wait – it was just sex. That's all it was, right? I catch myself asking this question with uncertainty.

What is going on? Is there more to it? No. I don't let myself ponder this any longer as I turn the water up hotter and let it burn my skin. I burn away the stupid idea of it being anything else. I convince myself – it's the lack of sleep talking. I fall asleep seeing those blues eyes piercing my soul.

# *Chapter 6*

I wake up and throw on some clothes. I message Nick. *"Hey what's up?"*

She instantly replies. *"Nothing, u?"*

*"Breakfast?"*

*"Yeah. Sure,"* she replies.

At Denny's we take our usual booth in the back. I look at my friend and notice she looks tired. "I didn't wake you did I?"

"No."

"What's wrong Nick?"

"I heard about your little episode last night."

I shrug.Stacy must have told her about last night. *She talks entirely too much* I think to myself.

"You have got to learn to treat people better," she chides.

Rolling my eyes I say, "She's a grown woman. I didn't force her to sleep with me."

The waitress comes over and interrupts Nick's comments. "Hello ladies. Can I start you off with something to drink?" She's smiling a little too hard at me and I smile back. Nick just rolls her eyes.

"I'll have a sweet tea," Nick says.

"Sprite."

"Do you know what you're going to order?" the woman asks directing her focus on me completely ignoring Nick. Nick clears her throat and tosses the woman a nasty glance.

"I'll have pancakes, scrambled eggs and bacon," Nick mutters off in a nasty tone. The woman writes down her order quickly looking bored.

"And what can I get you sweetie?" The woman looks in my direction and leans over enough for me to see down her shirt. I take in a full look and wink at her.

"Toast and scrambled eggs please."

"Is that all you want?" she asks leading me to believe she's not talking about the menu. I look her up and down, "Maybe I'll take something a little later," I say. She smiles and walks away. I check out her ass the whole time.

Nick kicks my leg under the table.

"Ow. What the fuck was that for?" I whine bending down to rub where she kicked me.

"Those wandering eyes is what has gotten you into the mess you got in last night," she growls at me.

"Whatever."

The sad part is, I know she's telling me the truth but I don't care. I can't. The waitress comes over to our table with our drinks. I look at her name tag and see her name is Donna. "Thank you Donna," I say sweetly.

"You're welcome."

Nick doesn't say anything. She clears her throat and Donna leaves the table.

"That was rude Nick."

"So what? Let's be honest. I might as well be invisible with the way she's undressing you with her eyes."

I chuckle and shake my head. Eager to change the subject, I ask her, "How's work going?" I really don't feel like listening to her chastise me.

"Man," she pouts. "I'm so tired of that place."

"Why don't you leave?" I ask.

"Not all of us are as privileged as you and don't have to work".

Anger flashes across my face and I cut my eyes at her responding, "If I could have my mother back I would take that over the money."

"Sky, - I'm sorry. I didn't think before I said that."

My mother passed away when I was sixteen. Burying her was one of the hardest things I've ever had to do. She became ill and I took care of her until she couldn't hold on anymore.

Once my mother died the world as I knew it would never be the same. Even though I had learned early how dark and lonely the world felt, I would experience how truly dark and lonely it is after losing my mother. I became used to it, or at least I pretend to. Brushing off her apology I changed the subject.

"Come out with me tonight. Drinks on me!" my anger momentarily forgotten.

"Ok," she says.

"Cool." Donna comes back over to the table with our food and my mouth waters. "Thanks," I say.

"Anything for you baby," she purrs.

Annoyed, Nick asks for a side of ketchup. Donna rolls her eyes and says, "Sure." She practically throws the ketchup on the table and walks away.

"Well there goes your tip bitch," Nick mumbles.

"As if you were going to tip anyway. I always do," I say smartly.

"Shut up jerk," she says stuffing her mouth full of pancakes. I rub my hands together and eat my toast.

***

Later on that night I'm looking through my closet when I hear a knock at the door.

"Coming," I shout. I run to the door in only my red boy shorts and look through the peephole. Nick is making a goofy face and I yank the door open.

"You're stupid you know that?" I say in a joking tone.

"Gross, go put some damn clothes on. I didn't want to see that." She yells as I walk away. I shake my hips and say, "Yes you did, I know you want me."

"In your dreams sweetheart."

A few moments later I walk back out buttoning up my shirt. "Ta Da," I say with my arms out spinning around in front of her.

"That's better. Let's go moron."

"I love you too," I say.

# *Chapter 7*

In the bar, Nick is dancing seductively in front of me while I bust out laughing hysterically. She keeps grinding her butt into my crotch and I can't help but entertain what she's doing.

Stacy comes over and gets behind me making me into a human sandwich. Laughing she grasps my waist and grinds herself into my butt.

"Are you guys' serious right now?" The music speeds up and so do their actions. I hear sucking of the teeth and turn to see Casey shaking her head at me.

Breaking free from Nick and Stacy I walk over and say, "Please don't throw a drink on me. They are just having fun." She rolls her eyes and orders a drink.

"Yeah, whatever you say."

Wondering why I even care what she thinks I take a seat next to her. "Listen, about that night. I'm sorry."

"Don't worry about it, I don't care."

"Obviously you do or you wouldn't have thrown a drink on me."

She turns glaring at me and says, "What is your problem anyway? Was I just another notch on your belt?"

"Something like that," I mumble and instantly regret it.

Stunned, she stares at me and slaps my face. I don't move. I grind my teeth. I can feel my cheek burning. Anger flares in me for a second until I look into her eyes.

They are hurt and sad. She slams money on the bar, turns and walks out. Nick comes over and asks if I'm alright.

"Yeah. Sure. Just my pride, I guess." I order another drink and put my head down on the bar.

"What happened?" she asks.

I shrug not giving her any answers.

Gulping down our drinks, Nick turns to me and says, "Let's walk around for a while." She takes my hand and doesn't wait for an answer.

We walk out into the cool night air. I can feel it loosen up my bones and mind. I look up at the night sky breathing in the air.

"She asked if she was just another notch for me and I said 'yeah' or something like that. I didn't really mean to say it out loud but I swear she brings out the worst in me."

Nick is silent listening to me rant on about how stupid I think Casey is and how childish she behaves. Clearing her throat she gives me a look that says she's not the only one.

"What? I was trying to be nice to her."

Still she says nothing.

"Ok, I was wrong for saying what I said but geez." The conversation dies and I'm left with my thoughts.

***

After driving Nick home I wander around in my car for a while feeling restless. Somehow I end up at Casey's house. Getting out of the car, I walk to the elevator.

## *Chapter 8*

I don't allow myself to question what I'm doing here. When I arrive at her door, I realize this is stupid and walk away. Then, I turn back and knock on the door.

I hear someone shuffling around with the locks and the door opens. She stands there staring at me like I have three heads.

She looks like I woke her because she is wearing a spaghetti strapped shirt that looks two sizes too small and a pair of boxer shorts. Casey rubs her eyes and yawns.

"What the hell are you doing here?"

I shrug. I'm tipsy and she can tell. She opens the door a little more and lets me through. Once inside I turn to her and try to formulate what to say.

At a loss for words I grab her, pull her to me and kiss her. I must have scared her because she tenses and eventually kisses me back. We kiss hard until there is no breath left in our lungs and have to break apart.

I lean my forehead against hers and whisper, "I want you."

She doesn't say anything but takes my hand and leads me to the bedroom. This time I actually take a look around. Her bedroom is plush. She has a sheer canopy around the bed and the walls all have abstract paintings lining them. There are candles all over the place making the room look romantic.

I turn to her and pull her against me. We stare into each other's eyes. I can read the hunger and lust in hers. I want this woman. She has a power over me that I can't shake loose. Do I want to shake it loose? I don't answer my mind as I pull her into a deep kiss.

Her mouth is warm and soft. I can't seem to get enough of it. I push my tongue deeper into her mouth and make her take what I have to offer. She willingly accepts and sucks on my lips.

She pulls my shirt from my jeans and unbuttons it. The buttons take too long for me so I rip the offending shirt away from my body.

Buttons fly in all sorts of directions. This makes her hungrier and she yanks my pants open and down my legs. I pull her shirt and boxer shorts off in a hurry.

We stumble into the bed. On top of her I gaze down at her as I lower my body on hers. Her mouth forms a perfect "O" as our skin touches. We are on fire. It feels as though the flames will burn us alive.

I lower myself until there is no barrier between us. I take her lips again. She moans into my mouth.

Lying there, a rush of emotions from deep within comes over me and covers my skin. The moans, murmurs, and whispers drive my body into unbelievable frenzy. I cannot regain control. Caresses and touches pull me into her darkness.

I'm blinded and frightened. I cannot see. I can only hear the hunger building. She pulls, digs and scratches at anything she can get her hands on.

The marks left behind are the only indication that this is real.  We fight the release, working with all of our might to prolong the inevitable.  It becomes a losing battle as our bodies glide higher and higher until the blinding light is all we see.

We plunge into that piercing light and take it for all it is. Even after we have fed that hunger, it beckons for more. It calls and calls until at last we must answer.

Hearts racing, breath coming fast, we fall again into the bliss that has become us. Then something changes.

The pace slows. What seemed like a hunger quickly turns into a need. A need to feel. A need to touch. A need to belong.

As our bodies come together for that final kiss, our eyes lock. Hearts that once beat separately now beat as one. We cry out one final time knowing that the thirst has been quenched. At least for now.

Looking over at her body splayed across the bed, the sheets leave her back exposed. I'm stricken with panic. I feel it rising, causing my body to sweat.

Do I have feelings for her? My hands crave the touch of her bare skin one more time, but I don't. I get up and dress.

I leave her and run away from what she represents. Her intensity is overbearing and I can't handle what she quietly demands from me. Running from her apartment is all I know how to do. I don't know how to love her. *I won't love her* I tell myself. I can't let that happen.

I snatch a cigarette, light it and pull the smoke into my lungs until they burn and scream. This brings me back to my comfort zone.

Driving away, I leave her and all she offers behind. If only life was that simple and I could stay in a bubble with her. This world is dark and harsh. Full of hurt, regrets, mistakes and loss.

# *Chapter 9*

I won't pretend that things are good and happy, because they aren't. Not for me. Nothing has ever been good for me and I accepted this a long time ago.

Weeks pass. I dare not go to the bar. Instead, I am a coward and don't leave my comfort in the dark. I stay inside and drink until I no longer see her piercing blue eyes haunting me. I no longer feel her on my skin. I no longer feel my heart ache at what she has to offer.

Angrily, I throw my drink across the room and curse. It shatters on the floor with a loud chime.

"I hate you!"

What has she done to me? I don't want to feel. I want to go back to the way things were before. Again I drink, drowning my pain. The pain she has caused.

Bang! Bang!

A loud knock on the door jolts me out of my thoughts. I don't move. I don't breathe. I hear the lock being fumbled with and relax.

Nick. She is the only person with a key to my apartment. I pour a new drink and down it in one large gulp.

"Don't turn on the light," my voice croaks scratchy and dry. She doesn't and walks over to the couch. She sits and stares at me in the dark. I don't look up. I can't bear to see the emotions in her eyes that I know are there.

"Have you eaten?"

I shrug.

"How long have you been like this?"

Again I shrug. She takes the cup from my hand and pulls me to my feet. She drags me down the hall and turns the shower on in the bathroom. She undresses me and pushes me forward into the shower.

Inside the shower, the water burns my skin but I don't flinch. I don't care at this point. After a few moments I become emotional and collapse, sliding down into the tub.

Nick peers inside and says, "Honey what's the matter?"

I don't say anything. She climbs into the shower fully dressed and takes my naked body into her arms. I break. I sob heavily. She holds onto me for dear life.

*I'm in my dark place and there aren't any people. There is only me and the shadows. My dark place protects me from this thing we call life. In my dark place I don't have any expectations placed on me. It is just me. I don't have to pretend to be someone I'm not.*

*I can be myself and not worry about the judgment so many people have about the things I've done. In my dark place there are no hurt and no feelings, just a place to rest my mind which forever torments me. My dark place is like a hole in the ground that goes on and on forever.*

*There is loud, sad music playing and the voice singing sounds as if the worst of the hurt is in them. I grab onto that hurt and hold it as if it could disappear. This hurt is my comfort. It is the only thing that seems to be real.*

*I cut my arms and I feel free. The sting is so far in the back of my mind it does not register. The blood seeps out of the cuts and runs like a stream into a lake. I lift my arms and watch it run. The flow seems free to run on any path it decides. If only life was this simple. Instead there are signs and roads and people telling you which way you can and can't go.*

*My blood flows downward spilling onto the ground. Again I cut, just to see what path it chooses this time. As I look, the shadows come. Anger flares and I curse, for that's all I can do. These shadows haunt me and taunt me. They laugh when I think things are getting better. They block my path and keep me going where they desire me to go.*

*I try so very hard to move away from them but they are everywhere and nowhere at the same time. Their voices manifest as a mix of jumbled words most of the time that I don't understand. At other times the voices are saying things like "what is the point? You are a failure, why don't you cut yourself again?"*

*I turn the music up louder and try to drown them out. They become angry and tap my shoulder. When I turn to look no one is there. Then they grab my hair. I run my hands through my hair only to realize that nothing is there. Again they tap my shoulder. I scream, "What do you want?"*

*The only sounds are the echo of my voice. Am I losing it? Am I imagining this? What is happening to me? I feel as though there are billions and billions of words in my head and I can't make any sense of them. It is like a never ending sentence that just keeps playing over and over and over.*

*I realize I'm crazy and losing my mind. I'm falling in love with a woman and it scares the crap out of me. What am I going to do? Nothing. I make my mind up I will be a coward and do nothing about it. That's final.*

Weak, with no more tears to cry, we stand up. Nick lathers my body, rinses me off and turns the shower off. She towels me gently. We don't speak. Nick knows me better than anyone in this world.

Silence. That's what I need. Pulling me forward, she lays me in the bed that I rarely sleep in and pulls the covers over us both. Darkness envelopes my body. I'm asleep instantly.

***

When I awake, I sit up and yawn. I look down and notice I don't have any clothes on. I frown. My memory struggles to remember what happened. I glance around the room. I close my eyes and rest my head against the headboard. It all comes flooding back to me.

The drinks. The tears. The hot water and Nick. I hold my head in my hands. "I must be losing my mind," I say. Pushing the covers aside, I stand on shaky legs. There is a throbbing in my head and my mouth feels dry. I stumble to the dresser and pull on some shorts and a shirt. I head for the bathroom.

In the mirror, my eyes are red and swollen. Rubbing them, I reach for my toothbrush. I quickly brush my teeth and run a hand through my hair trying to tame my curls. I walk into the kitchen and hear the front door open.

"You're alive I see," Nick says.

"Mmmm," I grumble.

"Well, I brought you some coffee and some bagels."

I walk to her and kiss her lips. "I love you," I murmur.

"I know you do," she says. She hesitates. She appears to want to say something.

I stop her with my hand and say, "Let me eat first please." She must see the pleading in my eyes because she says nothing, walks over to the table and sets our food down. We eat in silence. I'm lost in my thoughts.

After finishing our food we move over to the couch. I sit, close my eyes and lean back. Waiting.

"What's the matter Sky?" Nick asks in a low voice.

"I don't know." I turn to her. She looks into my eyes and I know she can see it.

"You have feelings for her." She states this rather than asks the question. Instantly I jump up off the sofa and start pacing.

"Why did she have to move here anyways? Why did I sleep with her? What does she want from me?" I continue to rant and Nick stays quiet. After I've run my course, I sit back down and Nick speaks.

"So you have feelings for her? What's so bad about having feelings for her?"

I glare at her and if looks could kill, Nick would be dead right now. Maybe I could just kill them both. That eliminates my problems. Laughing in my head I think I wouldn't be able to live without my best friend.

"There is nothing wrong with having feelings."

"Shut up!" I scream. "If you say feelings one more time, you are leaving." She looks as though she is going to challenge me. I stand my ground. She thinks better of it and says nothing.

Quietly she asks, "What are you going to do about it?"

"WHAT? Nothing. I'm not going to do anything about it. It will pass," I say not sounding so sure.

"So you're just going to hide in the house forever?" she asks incredulously.

"No. Yes," I say, feeling ashamed of myself. "I don't know," I say in a frustrated tone.

"Well, I think that you should get to know her."

I think she must have lost her mind. I remain silent and she takes it as a sign that she's gone too far. She stands up and stretches.

"I have to go."

"Ok." I walk her to the door. After a caring hug, she walks away. I am left alone with my thoughts once again. I don't know what to do. I drum my fingers against my head and think.

Maybe I could go see her. No. What would I say? I snatch my keys off the table and head out the door. I drive to the nearest park and open the trunk of my car. I grab my basketball.

## *Chapter 10*

Basketball is my favorite sport. As much as I love to watch it, I also enjoy playing it. Dribbling the ball on the court I feel free. The courts are deserted. I feel even better. I see children laughing and running around the playground. I look at them with envy wishing my life were that simple again – I mean before I could feel anything.

I know how farfetched that is. I see a man dressed in workout clothes doing push-ups. He looks strong with bulging arms. Further past him there are two women walking the track at a furious pace. They both have on tight black shorts and tight tank top shirts. One woman has a headband around her head.

They are talking and walk past me. One of the women looks back at me and winks. I close my eyes and continue my trek to the courts. The courts have two basketball hoops on them. There is a black old-looking fence surrounding the court. This is a failed attempt at keeping the balls out of the little lake sitting behind the court.

I chuckle as I look at the water. I count six balls floating around. *So much for the fence* I think sarcastically. Once on the court, I shed my tee shirt leaving me in basketball shorts and my tank. I place my ball on the ground and stretch my muscles. Once I'm satisfied, I pick the ball up and run, dribbling the ball around the court.

I feel my breath becoming faster and it feels great. Wind blows my curls around my head. It reminds me that I need to get my air cut. I finish my slight run and I begin shooting the ball in the basket. The first five shots hit their mark perfectly. It takes my mind to another place.

*I am 15 and playing basketball for school. I am a terrible academic student but a hell of an athlete. Basketball is my sport of choice. It's where I shine. The basketball court is my second home. At times, it's better than home. Its lined boxes are where I have control and everyone loves me.*

*Since I struggle with my classes, I have to study hard and get extra help. With some discipline and the extra help, I am able to remain on the team.*

*My history teacher likes me and is always helping me. Mrs. K is the reason I am able to stay on the team. On the days that I don't have practice, I usually stay after class or go to her house for tutoring. Sometimes, it is more than tutoring.*

*Don't go there I tell myself.*

*I remember the day she told me that she was interested in me. It scared me but I liked her too. She would touch me inappropriately and cry and say how sorry she was. I never told anyone about this. I allowed it to continue all through school. Who was I going to tell anyways?*

*My mom was sick and depressed all the time. I felt as though she didn't need the extra stress. So I stayed quiet. Playing basketball was my release for everything that was going wrong in my life. Nothing else mattered when I was on the court.*

*Playing basketball was my life support. I needed it to survive. Honestly, basketball was my ticket out of this hell hole. Scouts were already noticing me and the possibilities excited me. None of my family ever came to my games, just Nick. She never missed a game. We had made it to the finals and I couldn't wait for the game.*

*I scanned the gym before the game and noticed the crowd. It never made me nervous. Nothing could touch me out there on the court. No feelings. No hurt, no pain. No people. Just me, doing what I loved to do. When the game started I felt at my best. I knew we were going to win. No matter what, I would make sure of it.*

*I remember dribbling the ball and I call out a play to my teammates. I pass off to the other guard and set up to shoot a three pointer. The ball is passed to me. I hold it and get a good look at the hoop. I arch and shoot the ball. Swish!*

*The crowd gets on their feet chanting us on. I run up the court and get ready for defense. Holding the opposing team member with a hand on her back, I go for the steal. Taking the ball away, one of my teammates hauls ass up the court. I pass the ball and she scores. The screams from the crowd get louder.*

*I clasp her hand in a congratulatory slap and we run up the court. I glance over at the scoreboard and see that we are winning by double digits. It's the fourth quarter with five minutes left in the game. I think to myself that this is going to be a piece of cake. Smiling, I ready myself for defense.*

*I steal the ball again. I race up the court. The crowd is on their feet. The moment is intense. I decide I'm going to dunk the ball for the crowd. Dribbling through defenders, I successfully make it to the goal.*

*I prepare to jump. I pick the ball up. I take a step. I launch myself into the air on my way to dunking the ball.*

*In my peripheral vision I see a defender sprinting to get to me. I pay her little attention. I'm about to score the winning slam dunk. I stretch myself higher to the goal. I feel the ball sliding through the hoop. Already cheering, I am caught off guard by my body being pushed in the other direction.*

*"What the-?"*

*My words are cut off by the loud crack I hear. My tail bone slams into the floor. Intense pain shoots through my body. My ankle cracks as well. I don't know which part to grab first. My head hits the ground last. Everything goes black.*

*I wake up hurting all over. My head throbs. My ankle feels like it's been torn off. My back and butt feel as though there are knives lodged in them. I mumble as I look around. I hear all sorts of beeping coming from a machine that's giving me oxygen.*

*I struggle to lift my arm and pull the mask off. I successfully pull it off and look down to see a cast on my ankle. There is a huge bandage wrapped around my head. "What the hell happened?" I say out loud.*

I cringe and shake the memory from my head. Anger takes over. I drive the ball from one hoop to the other at a furious pace. Sweating and panting I grab the ball and launch it over the fence.

"Fuck!" I scream at the top of my lungs. I don't care what people may think. I climb up the fence to retrieve my ball. The metal fence slices through my arm. I pay little attention to the pain as I continue to climb over the fence.

I hit the ground with a thud and it makes my head spin. Wiping blood away, I finally reach my ball. I pick it up and head back over the fence. Looking at the basketball hoop I see my dreams and hopes that faded away from me. They fell right through my hands it seems.

Basketball was the only thing I could trust and truly believe in. Basketball was the one thing that hadn't hurt me. Basketball was my savior from all the hurt and pain I had endured.

Cursing under my breath, I briskly stride back to my car. I slam the door and speed off, burning tires as I rev the engine up. Hitting the gas I speed through town not really paying attention to where I'm going. I end up at Casey's apartment and don't really know why.

Not thinking about it much, I get out the car and ride the elevator up to where she is. Once there, I cautiously knock on the door.

## *Chapter 11*

I hear nothing at first. Then, finally, the door opens. She looks startled as if she is surprised it was me knocking on the door. Her eyes widen. Panic crosses her features.

"What the fuck happened to you?" she says. She doesn't wait for me to reply as she pulls me through the door. She pulls me into the bathroom and firmly places me on the toilet. She rummages through the cabinets searching for her first aid kit I assume.

"Basketball," I mumble.

"What?" She asks.

"I hurt myself playing basketball." I know that's not really the truth but it's not all a lie.

"Oh." She's quiet as she cleans my face where I'd inadvertently smeared blood from my arm. She presses the towel a little hard against my arm and I say, "Ow!" and pull away a little.

"I'm sorry," she says but doesn't seem like she really means this.

"It's ok,"

She cleans my arm and I take the time to study her. She has on glasses that I've not noticed before. She's mumbling while she cleans the nasty cut on my arm. She looks so beautiful my breath is momentarily taken from me. Her skin is tanned and she looks young with hair falling into her face.

I ache to touch her. To tell her I'm sorry. To do something to undo what I've done to hurt her already. Lost in my own thoughts I hadn't noticed she had finished. She turns away from me to the sink and washes her hands.

"I think you need stitches," she says in a motherly tone.

"Na. It will be ok," I say not really caring about my arm.

We are in her tiny bathroom and suddenly it feels as though there isn't enough space. I need to get away from her but I stay. She senses this at the same time and slides past me.

I can tell she's trying not to touch me but fails as her leg rubs against my skin. I close my eyes as the sensations run over me and settle in my stomach.

I stand and trap her against the wall. We stare at each other. Seconds turn into minutes and we stand there not moving. I want to kiss her but I keep myself still. I fear her rejection. Does she want me as much as I want her? Can she see that I have feelings for her?

Clearing her throat she breaks the silence. She escapes from underneath my arm, and walks away from me. I draw a deep breath and follow her into the living room. We take a seat and she asks if I would like anything to drink.

"Alcohol?" I question.

"Sure," she says. She comes back with a bottle of vodka and a cup of ice. I twist the top off and pour a generous amount in the cup. Settling down she watches as I gulp down half of my drink. The vodka burns my throat but I welcome the feeling.

"So…were you in the neighborhood?" she asks sarcastically.

I roll my eyes and glare at her. "No. I wanted to see you." My response takes her by surprise because she just sits there with her mouth hanging open.

She recovers and says, "Oh."

I pour another drink and gulp it down. *My liquid courage* I think to myself. I set my glass down, turn and look at her. She's beautiful. Her skin is flawless.

I slide closer to her and pull her into a kiss.  She pulls me on top of her. I kiss her more frantically. Our breathing is ragged and we break apart for more air.

I leave her wonderful mouth and kiss her neck. I leave a trail of kisses from her neck to her ear. I push my pelvis into hers and hear her moan. Taking that as a good sign, I grind against her harder. She arches and moans louder.

"I can't do this," she pants and pushes me away.

She slides from underneath me. Her skin is flushed and her breathing is fast. I can see her chest heaving up and down. Her lips are swollen from our kissing. "I can't do this with you again, I'm sorry."

I'm at a loss as to what I should say. "I can tell you want me just as much as I want you," I say breathless.

"That's not the point. I can't keep doing this with you. I can't keep getting hurt every time you leave. I need someone who is going to be there for me. Not just want to have sex with me."

I work to formulate a thought. Nothing comes out.

"That's what I thought." She bends down and writes on a piece of paper. She hands me the paper and says, "Call me when you're ready for something other than sex."

I stand and take the paper from her. Without another glance I walk to the door, open it and continue through it. Walking to my car I feel numb. I look up at Casey's window and stare. I don't know what to do. Should I go back and give her what she wants? I can't. I know that.

I feel the frown on my face. I start the car and drive away. I drive, all the while thinking about what took place. I can still feel my body against hers. I tremble at the feeling.

"Damn," I mutter trying to shake the thoughts from my head. Once at my apartment, I unlock the door and walk inside. I slam myself on the couch and bury my head in the pillows.

## *Chapter 12*


I can't understand why this is happening to me. What makes her so different than anyone else?

My thoughts are halted by a knocking at the door. I struggle up from my slump and I answer the door. Valerie stands there looking good as ever. She struts into the apartment with a huge smile on her face.

Breathing deeply, I realize I don't really feel like company. This surprises me and also catches me off guard.

"Hey sexy," she says and runs her hands up and down my stomach. Noticing the bandage on my arm she asks what happened.

"Oh nothing," I lie and shrug it off. I back away from her touch but she continues anyway. She kisses me roughly and tries to push me backwards to the sofa. I grab her harder than I mean to and hold her away from me.

"Not now," I say. She looks at me with questioning eyes. I try to recover and say that I'm not feeling well.

"You look well to me," she grins.

"Yeah, well I'm not really feeling up to company," I say firmly.

She sucks her teeth and grabs her purse. "Whatever. Call me when you want to fuck?"

I don't say anything as she leaves. I close the door and bang my head against the frame. I do this again as if it will change the way I feel. It doesn't.

I grab a sweater and head out the door. In the bar I see Nick and Stacy kissing behind the bar. I roll my eyes and make a loud disgusting sound. They break apart.

"Hey," Nick says and walks over to me. She hugs me and asks what happened to my arm.

"I hurt myself playing ball."

She doesn't look convinced but leaves it at that. Thankfully, Stacy walks over and hands me a drink. Nick tells her I hurt my arm playing ball and I look over at her and suck my teeth.

"What?" she asks sarcastically. "I was trying to save you from having to tell what happened twice."

I slap her arm playfully and say, "Right. I'm sure that's what you were doing. Thank you."

"You are such a sarcastic prick, you know that."

I smile wide and give her the best charming smile I can muster. "That's why you love me," I say.

A dark cloud passes over my face and Nick senses something is up. "What's wrong?" she asks tentatively.

"Nothing. Well, I went to Casey's house again."

"WHAT!" She practically screams at me. Other people in the bar look over at us and our antics. We pay them little attention as Nick asks in a lower voice this time, "What happened?"

I shrug and tell her, "I don't know why I even went there. She cleaned up my cuts and made me a drink. We were sitting on the sofa and one thing led to another."

"Did you have sex with her again?"

"No. She ended up stopping things and I just left."

"You have got to talk to her."

I know Nick is right but I don't even know where to start. "I don't even know what it is that I want from her". I look up at Nick with questioning eyes.

"I know, but maybe if you guys sit down and talk about things you can come to a conclusion. It would be a good place to start." Nick finishes.

"Maybe." I let what Nick has said settle in my mind. I think it would be a good place for us to start. Maybe if I could explain to her my side of things she would better understand me.

As I drink, I allow my mind to wander. I close my eyes. I see Casey staring up at me, asking me to give myself to her. My body aches at the thought of touching her again.

Later that evening back at home, I take out the paper she gave me. I know what I need to do. I text her.

"Hi, it's Sky. I was wondering if you could meet me at my place or go out to eat so that we can talk."

It feels like a lifetime before I hear my phone buzz. Excited, I pick it up and look at the screen.

"Hi. We can meet at Friday's if you want."

Disappointed that she turned down my invitation to come to my place but glad she has agreed to meet up with me, I text back.

"Ok. Friday's sounds good. When?"

"Tomorrow for lunch around noon or so?" Casey responds

"Sure sounds good to me." I text.

"K" she responds.

I don't really know what else to text so I say, "See you at noon then."

"Yep."

"See you there."

I place my phone on the table and feel my heart rate increase. What am I going to say to her? What will she say to me? I drive myself crazy with questions and lay my head back and drift off to sleep.

The next morning I wake up feeling sore and tired. Last night was a rough night. I feel as though I didn't get any sleep.

I can't stop myself from thinking about my lunch with Casey. I stand and stretch. My muscles protest the whole time.  I rub the sore spots and fail to make them feel any better. I go and get in the shower. I let the hot water stream over my body and it begins to loosen up my muscles. I sigh at how good the water feels and put my face into the spray.

The water cascades all over my head. I shampoo my hair. Bathing my body and rinsing off, I step out of the shower dripping wet. As I snag my towel and dry off, I notice a huge bruise on my ribs. I run my hand over the bruise and realize I must have hurt myself worse than I thought.

I wrap the towel around my waist and wipe the dew off the mirror. As I stare at myself, my eyes look sharp and clear for the limited amount of rest I've gotten. Leaning down and brushing my teeth, I start to feel human. I hum out loud and go into my bedroom to search for clothes to put on.

I feel so giddy. I'm thinking that it has something to do with meeting up with Casey. Rummaging through my drawers, I find what I'm looking for and put my underclothes on.

I saunter to the closet and slip on my navy cargo shorts and dark pink polo.

Satisfied with how my outfit looks, I go back in the bathroom to try and tame my messy hair.

I pad into the living room barefoot and search for my white loafers. I forgo socks and put my shoes on and pick up my phone. It's already eleven. I need to get a move on if I want to show up on time. I tidy up the place and take one last look before I head out the door.

It's hot and humid outside and doesn't take long for me to break a sweat. Mumbling about how Florida's weather sucks, I get into my car and crank the air conditioning on high. I pull on my seatbelt and slip out onto the road.

# *Chapter 13*

I arrive at Friday's ten minutes early. I even take the time to straighten my clothes. Satisfied with my look, I pull out a cigarette and smoke quickly. I am nervous.

I consider whether or not I should cancel but then I hear a voice in my head saying, "You're a coward." I clear my throat and stub out my cigarette. I proceed to the entrance. "I can do this," I chant under my breath.

At the door, I notice a lady struggling to get her baby in a stroller. Cursing that good

side to me, I go over and ask if she needs
help.

"Please!" she says in a desperate voice.
She hands her baby to me. I'm caught off
guard.

I hold the baby away from me
awkwardly. The baby smiles and squirms in
my arms. I straighten up and hold the baby
better.

She smiles up at me and places her
small chubby fingers on my face. I can't
help myself. I smile back at the little one.
Her fat cheeks are wet from her slobber. I
think to myself how gross that is.

After a moment, the woman has the
stroller fixed and takes the baby from my
arms. "Thank you," she says out of breath.

"You're welcome," I reply and walk off
before she tries to hand the baby over to me

again. I hold the door open for her and the baby and she pushes the stroller through it.

Inside the restaurant is nice and cool and I'm thankful for the air conditioning. The place is small and cramped and noisy. There are people everywhere.

Workers are coming in and out of a door in the back leading to the kitchen. I search around the dining area for Casey but don't see her. I take in a deep breath as a woman comes over and asks, "How many?"

"Two," I respond.

"Would you like a table or a booth?" she asks.

"A booth will be fine," I say politely.

I follow her to the middle and notice that most of the people eating here are on their phones. Even the people I see are here on dates are paying more attention to their phones than their dates.

Shaking my head, I say to myself *this is what life has become*. Entertainment. With Facebook, Instagram, and all of the other social media sites people can't live without.

The woman seats me and I look up at her. She is an older woman, maybe in her late fifties with black/graying hair. Her cheeks are red and her face is round. She looks good for her age and I can tell that in her younger years she must have been a real looker.

"Can I start you off with a drink?" The woman asks.

Glancing at the menu in front of me I try to see what I want.

"Hmmm I'll take a strawberry daiquiri," I say.

The woman lets me know that they are two for one and it excites me.

"Did you want to put in an appetizer or wait on your guest to arrive?"

I order some nachos in case she is running late. The woman takes down my order and leaves the table. Before she returns, Casey walks through the door.

It's as if everything stops and she and I are the only ones there. I watch her glide effortless towards me. God this woman takes my breath away. Her eyes shine and her smile makes me feel warm and tingly inside.

She's wearing a short, tight red dress with black heels. She has a gold necklace around her neck and earrings to match. She's beautiful. Casey slides into the booth and says, "Hello."

"Hi!" I say and my throat is dry. Just then the waitress comes and places my drink in front of me. I take a large sip and dry to quench my thirst.

Let's be honest. It's not my drink I want in my mouth. It's Casey. I shake the thought from my head and observe as Casey orders a sex on the beach. I cock my right brow at her and smile.

She shrugs her shoulders innocently and feigns a look of boredom. Again I smile. She lets the waitress know that the nachos will be fine for now.

"Thank you for coming," I belt out.

"Thanks for inviting me."

Not knowing what else to say I pick my drink up staring at her intensely.

"What? Do I have something on my face?" She asks.

"No. Just staring at how beautiful you are," I say with confidence.

She blushes and looks down and away from me. The waitress comes back to the table and places Casey's drink in front of her. She places the nachos in between us both.

"Thank you," we say at the same time. Smiling I say, "Sorry."

"S'ok" she says.

The waitress walks off shaking her head at us. Not paying attention, we both reach for the nachos at the same time. Electricity shoots up my arm and we stare at each other. Reluctantly, I pull my hand back. "Go ahead."

Casey takes some nachos and puts them on her plate. When she is finished I follow suit.

"How's your arm?"

"As good as new," I lie.

"That's good. I was a little worried about you last night."

"So you were thinking about me last night?" I quirk my brow.

Smiling she says "No, I was thinking about your injuries."

"Sure, tell yourself that's all you were thinking about. I know otherwise."

She laughs. "I don't know how you can stand to live next to your ego."

I put my hands on my chest and feign hurt. I pout.

"Awww, put your lip back in, geez you're adorable when you pout."

I know I'm grinning too big. "I got the desired response I see."

She remains quiet but smiles. Casey picks up her fork and begins eating her food. I do the same. I stop myself from eating and look up at her.

"I'm sorry," I say.

She gives me a questioning glance. I clear my throat and try again.

"I'm sorry for hurting you the way I did."

She puts her fork down and stares at me. Finally she asks, "Why did you?"

I shrug and say, "I don't know." I realize she's not going to let me off easily. Breathing heavily I continue. "My life is simple and I like it that way. I don't get hung up on people. I don't like relationships." She just stares at me. I feel compelled to tell her my story and don't really understand why.

"I've had a lot of hurt and loss in my life. It's the only way I know how to protect myself," I finish in a shaky voice.

"Why do you assume I'll hurt you?" She questions.

"Doesn't everyone?" I say a little angry.

Stung by my words she retorts back, "I guess we should all be heartless and numb like you then?" I take a deep breath. I struggle to calm myself down.

"I'm sorry," she says in a quiet voice. "I don't know you or what you've been through," she finishes. I look at her with sad eyes, wishing we could start over. I realize stupidly that's not a possibility.

Feeling compelled again to tell her my story, I say, "My mother died when I was a kid and she was all I had left."

Casey looks at me, her eyes sad. She covers her mouth with her hand and says she's sorry. I brush her apology away.

"It's not your fault."

Changing the subject I ask her about her parents. She says they are still living but not in this state.

"Do you visit them often?" I ask.

Casey shrugs and says, "When I can."

"What do you do for a living?" I ask.

"I'm a nurse at the local hospital."

"Cool."

"You?" she asks.

"I'm disabled."

She looks confused.

"I got injured real badly in high school."

"Oh." She says. She blushes and I can tell what she's thinking.

"I make the best of what I have." I say laughing.

Raising her brows she states, "I see."

We grow quiet for a moment and I ask, "Would you like to go to the fair with me?"

She ponders my question for a moment and then says, "Sure."

Happy, we eat the rest of our meal in silence.

"So are you asking me out on a date?"

"Yes," I say sounding confident.

"Ok," she smiles.

We finish our meals. I pay and we head out the door. Outside, the sun is still glaring and Casey uses her hands to shield her eyes. I walk her to her car and she turns to me. She places a kiss gently on my lips and it leaves me wanting more.

"I'll text you later about the fair," she says.

"Ok," I say.

I open her car door and she gets in. I watch as she drives away. I jog to my car andget in. I allow the air conditioning to cool me off. I pick up my phone and dial Nick's number.

"Hello."

"We have a date!"

"Yeah?" She says expecting more details.

I run down what happened at lunch and she tells me she's proud of me. Beaming, I breeze through traffic and return home. I sit in the house skimming through TV channels and my mind wanders back to Casey and our conversation. I don't know why I felt so compelled to tell her what has happened in my life.

Because she's comfortable I conclude. It's easy to talk to her. I try to convince myself that's the only reason why but I know better. I don't really pay attention to what is on the TV screen.

My phone goes off. I Stretch and pick my phone up off the table. Looking at the text I see that Casey has said, "What time should we meet tomorrow?"

I respond back saying, "Around seven or so."

She answers me back with an, "OK. I'll meet you then."

I place my phone back on the table and lay back and drift off to sleep. My sleep is haunted with faces and voices. I jerk awake and sit up and wipe my eyes. I stumble sleepily to the shower.

Once inside the shower I let the water run over my skin. I turn the hot water way down and it turns cold. The shock to my senses gets the desired effect. When I feel more alive, I shake myself free of water and get out. Having bad dreams is something I've become accustomed to.

They rarely bother me anymore. I quickly brush my teeth and comb my hair and head into my bedroom. I step into my closet and search for what I want to wear later in the evening.

I grab clothes and throw them on the floor. I don't really pay attention to the mess I'm making. I continue scrambling through the closet until at last I grab what I want.

I trip over the mess I've made and put my clothes on the bed. With a deep breath, I pick up the clothes I haphazardly threw on the floor. Luckily, the day passes by quickly but not quick enough for me.

## *Chapter 14*

I have cleaned my apartment three times already. I'm about to scream when I get a message from Casey asking if we're still on. I quickly respond back yes.

I check the time and see it's time I get dressed. I iron my pants and put them on. I throw on a clean tank under my button up. I check myself in the mirror and grin at how good I look.

I buckle my belt and add the finishing touches to my looks. The search for my keys fortunately ends quickly. As I head out the door, I realize it's a little breezy out and am glad I decided to wear long sleeves and pants. I think to myself how crazy Florida's weather is.

I drive half an hour away from home to the fair. Finding parking is a bitch and I realize the place is packed.

"Probably a whole bunch of school kids," I mutter to myself. I get out of the car and throw some gum in my mouth.

I'm anxious as I walk to the front gate where we decided to meet. Casey has arrived before me and I instantly spot her. I slow my pace and take her in.

She is wearing black skinny jeans with a red sweater shirt. She looks good. I see her staring at me and it does wonders for my ego. *She is checking me out* I say to myself.

I come to a stop in front of her and nervously kiss her cheek and say, "Hello."

"Hi!" she says back.

I take her hand and we walk up to purchase our tickets.

"So I must tell you that I don't really like riding fair rides," I say quickly.

"Me either," she says. "But we have to ride the Farris wheel."

"Ok," I agree.

Taking her hand again, we walk through the gate. We stop and look at the large amount of people here. Children are running all over the place with parents trying to keep up. There are clowns performing tricks for the little ones. Smiling, I pull her over to the right where I see a basketball challenge.

"Step right up if you think you have what it takes," a man with a bad haircut says. I pay him and he hands Casey three basketballs. She looks at me with a questioning glance.

"You know this is the part where I should tell you I'm no good at sports," she says.

"Come on!" I cheer. "You can do it!"

Breathing in, she takes the ball and shoots it toward the hoop. It falls way short and I stifle a laugh.

"Come on Case You can do it!" I say, realizing I have given her a nickname. She doesn't seem bothered by it and tries again. The ball sails through the air and falls short of the hoop again. "Hold on," I say.

I walk over and stand behind her. I instantly become overwhelmed with her lovely scent. It is a mixture of flowers and something else, like honey. I close my eyes and breathe it in.

I hold her hips and steady her body to correct her stance. I run my hands down her arms and show her how to properly hold the ball.

I feel her tremble at my touch. I smile. Her breathing speeds up and I continue to caress her arms.

"Ok, when you get ready to shoot, push the ball toward the hoop with your dominant hand."

I make sure she shows me the motion before she tries again. Satisfied, I step back. Following my directions, she arches and shoots the ball towards the hoop. It sails through the air and bounces around the rim a couple of times before finally sinking through the hoop.

Casey jumps up and hoots and hollers about her made basket. She runs over to me and grabs me in a tight hug. I hug her back and congratulate her on her shot. She kisses my cheek.

"I'm sorry you have to make at least two shots to get a prize," the man boasts.

Casey looks defeated and I tell her I'll win something for her. I pay the man again. I get three basketballs.

Readying myself, I look at the rim and then at Casey. I look back at the hoop and pick the first ball up. I shoot it and it goes in with a swish.

Casey cheers me on. I shoot again and all you hear is swish. I pick up the last ball and shoot it one handed. It lands perfectly in the hoop. The man rolls his eyes at me.

I laugh and tell Casey to pick out her prize. She chooses a huge bird looking thing and we continue walking around. I stop and buy us a huge thing of cotton candy. Casey frowns at me but smiles.

"What's the fair without cotton candy?" I say sounding like a happy child.

She laughs as she takes some and puts it in my mouth. I swallow the sweet stuff and tear off a huge piece. I shove it in her mouth getting it all over her face.

"Come on! Gross!" she squeals.

I help her wipe it off. I tear another piece and feed it to her properly. She looks thankful.

"You're no fun," I pout poking my lip out.

"Oh no! Not the lip again."

Casey tears some off and smears it around my mouth. I laugh, feeling carefree for the first time in a long time. I wipe it off licking my fingers soundly.

We throw the rest away and prepare to get on the Farris wheel. Once seated, we wait for the ride to start. It doesn't go unnoticed that Casey takes a seat next to me instead of sitting on the other side.

I pull her closer to me and put my arm around her protectively. The ride starts and I feel my heart speed up. I was never a big fan of heights but being here with her makes me feel safe.

I am amazed at the city from up high. Everything is so beautiful. It's all lit up and the lights make the place look bigger than it is.

Casey and I lock eyes. We lean in at the same time. I close my eyes as our lips meet in a soft, slow kiss. The world behind us fades away as I only feel her lips on mine.

I place my hand on her cheek and deepen the kiss. We become lost in our kissing until I hear a man clearing his throat.

The ride has stopped and a couple of kids are giggling and pointing at us. Blushing, Casey breaks free from my grasp and I instantly feel the loss. I miss her body being with mine, her heat.

We step off the ride. I take her hand and we continue exploring the fair. Casey steps away to grab us a drink and I feel someone grab my shoulder.

My defenses instantly go up as I prepare to swing. I come face to face with Valerie and unclench my fists.

"Geez you scared me," I say.

"I'm sorry," she says and takes my mouth into a searing kiss.

In the distance I hear drinks crash to the ground. Breaking free from Valerie I look over in time to see Casey running away from me. I step out to follow but Valerie catches my arm.

"Where you going baby?" she whines.

I push her away and tell her I'm on a date. She finds this funny and laughs at me. Anger flaring I stare at her hard.

"I'm serious," I say in a tone that gets through to her.

"Oh god, you're for real?" She laughs and says, "It's not going to go anywhere anyways!"

"That's not for you to decide," I say angrily. "I don't want to see you anymore," I spit out at her and storm away.

I hear Valerie scream, "Fuck you!" but I continue to make my way through the crowd to Casey. I get to the gate entrance panting. I frantically look around.

She's nowhere to be seen. Defeated, I slump my shoulders and shuffle to my car.

# Chapter 15

I kick myself for what has taken place and drive to the bar. On the way there I have called Casey like ten times, but no answer. I leave her a message saying sorry and to please call me back.

I look around the bar and anger engulfs me because I don't see her here. I walk over and slam myself on a stool. Stacy comes over with a drink

"What's wrong?"

"I fucked up again."

"How?" she asks.

I tell Stacy what happened at the fair and look up at her when I finish. She flinches and says, "Damn. Maybe you should try calling her?"

"I did that already," I say, frustrated.

"Ok, maybe you should go over to her place and try to talk to her?"

Smiling I say, "That's a great idea."

I leave my drink on the bar and run out saying thank you. Stacy just smiles and shakes her head. I arrive at Casey's house at top speed and jump out of the car barely giving it time to stop. I'm impatient waiting on the elevator, so I decide to run up the stairs.

Out of breath I place my hands on my knees and try to calm down. After a while I feel better and walk up to her door.

I pound on the door and wait. Nothing. Pounding on the door again I say, "Come on Case, open the door."

I hear the door finally open and feel grateful.

"Go away!" she spits out angrily.

"Come on, I'm sorry. I didn't mean for that to happen."

Casey opens the door wider and steps out. She looks like she's been crying. Her eyes are swollen and red.

"Listen to me," she says. "I thought you could change but you can't. I'm not going to be stupid and keep getting hurt by what you do. I don't want to hear from you or see you, so please leave."

Hurt by her words, I try again to plead my case. She doesn't wait and listen. She just slams the door in my face.

I place my hand on the door and bang my head against it. I slide to the floor. My head drops and all I see is my lap. *Damn I've really screwed everything up this time.*

Minutes pass and I realize I need to leave. I force myself up and I brush myself off. I head back to my car.

I smoke five cigarettes before I make it home. I slam the door and fix myself a drink. I'm defeated and have no clue how to fix it. I drink myself to sleep.

## *Chapter 16*

When I wake up the next morning, I remember what has taken place and start drinking some more. I drink until I can no longer think straight. I drink until I start crying. Tears pour out of my eyes and my body begins to shake.

Why does everything have to go wrong for me? Why, when I finally decide to open myself up, does it backfire? Why does this always happen to me? I drink until I feel myself getting sick. I drink until I pass out.

Weeks pass with no word from Casey. She won't answer my calls or my knocks at her door. I continue to shut the world out and drink.

I don't answer Nick or Stacy when they call. I won't let them in the apartment. I have completely shut everyone out. More weeks pass. I continue on the same path.

Bang! Bang! Bang!

I hear pounding at my door and don't get up to answer it. I hear the locks being unlocked and I'm too weak to stop Nick from coming in.

"Geez look at you. You're a mess," she says in a frustrated tone.

"So, fucking what!" I spit out. "Why are you even here? Why don't you just leave?"

"I came to tell you that there's been an accident."

I sit up slightly interested. "What? With who?"

"Casey has gotten into an accident and it's bad."

I jump off the sofa and head out the door. Nick grabs my arm and yanks me back.

"You can't go anywhere looking like that! You need to clean yourself up."

Impatient, I look down at myself and agree. I haven't eaten or showered in I don't know how long. I shower at a blazing speed and get dressed.

"Ready," I come out saying.

Nick takes my keys and says, "I'm driving."

I don't argue with her. I just want to see

Casey. We get to the car and we speed off.

At the hospital I jump out of the car before

Nick has stopped and run inside.

# Chapter 17

"I need to see Casey Taylor," I say.

A woman looks up bored and says, "What's the person's name?

I yell at her. "My friend was brought here! Her name is Casey Taylor."

The woman types on the computer and nods her head. "If you'll follow me, I'll take you to her."

I have to concentrate to not to step on the woman's heels. I follow. We whiz through several halls and rooms until finally we reach Casey's room.

As I stand at the door, panic takes over. Casey is laying there, her face black and bruised. There are all sorts of tubes all over her.

The machine is beeping and she has a breathing tube in her mouth. Her left leg is in a sling and her right arm is in a cast. I place my hand over my mouth as tears well up in my eyes. I move slowly to the bed and kneel next to her.

I take her uninjured hand into mine and kiss it. The doctor comes in and asks who I am. I lie and say I'm her girlfriend and ask what her status is.

The doctor clears his throat and says, "Casey has sustained a pretty bad head injury due to her car accident. She has had surgery to bring down the swelling and bleeding. Right now she is in a drug induced coma due to her injuries. We will have to wait and see what happens before we can be sure of anything."

His words echo in my head. I finally look up at him and say thank you. He leaves the room. I move the chair closer to the bed and sit down. Before I have a chance to settle, the tears start. My tears turn into sobs as I cry out, devastated by what has happened.

Nick comes in and scoops me up out of the chair. "It's going to be alright honey," she soothes.

"No its not!" I say loudly. "I didn't even get a chance to tell her that I love her Nick! What if she doesn't wake up? How can I live with myself knowing that I love her and didn't get the chance to tell her?"

I break down completely and sob. The sobs rock my body and I crumble to the floor. Nick scoops me up and turns my face to hers. I try to pull away but her hand holds my face.

"Look at me," she admonishes in a stern voice. I look up at her.

"Casey is going to pull through this and you will get the chance to tell her how much she means to you. Ok?"

"You really think so?" I whisper in a small voice.

"Yes."

She sounds so sure that I want to believe her. I wipe the tears from my face and stand up straighter to get control of myself. I hear people coming into the room and I turn to see who it is.

An older man and woman walk in. The man is very handsome. He is tall and towers over me. The woman is an older version of Casey.

She has the same deep blue eyes and dark hair. *These must be Casey's parents* I say to myself. Feeling nervous I decide I'd better say hi.

"Hi, my name is Sky. I'm Casey's girlfriend," I say smoothly. I reach my hand out to them.

Nick rolls her eyes at me and covers her mouth to keep from laughing, I assume. I frown at her and continue to look at Casey's parents as they introduce themselves.

"Hi, I'm Bill, Casey's father," the man says in a deep voice.

I shake his hand and it's strong and firm. I turn to Casey's mother.

"Hi my name is Sue, I'm Casey's mother. I didn't realize Casey had a girlfriend. I don't remember her mentioning it to me," she says.

Sue pulls me into a strong hug, tears streaming down her face. Caught off guard, I become emotional and hug her back tight.

Nick clears her throat and I pull away to introduce her. "Bill, Sue, this is my best friend Nick."

They say hello and Nick tells me that she has to get back to work and to call her when I hear something. I hug her goodbye. Staring and shuffling around uncomfortably, I tell Casey's parents that I can give them some privacy.

"No sweetheart, that's not necessary. You're her girlfriend, I'm sure she wants you to be here too." Sue walks over to the bed and takes her daughter's hand.

"Oh baby what happened to you. Please pull through this honey. I know you are strong enough."

Bill joins his wife's side and also talks to Casey. I sneak out to the hallway to get some fresh air. Sitting on the bench, I place my head in my hands and do something I haven't done in a long time.

I pray. I plead and beg God to bring Casey back to me and her family. I plead for him not to take her away from me.

Crying and thinking I'm going to lose her, I hear her mom step out as well. She comes over and sits next to me. I brush the tears from my eyes and look up at her. She pulls me close and I wrap my arms around her. I close my eyes and allow my mind to wander to another time.

*I was fourteen and my dad was still gone. Coming home from school like I always did, I go through the house looking for my mom.*

*"Mom!" I call out. Nothing. "Mom!" I call again.*

*I become slightly scared. I frown and search the bedroom. I see my mom lying on the floor with blood pouring out of her mouth. Bending down, I put my hand on her neck but don't feel a pulse.*

*I grab my phone and dial 911. I wait impatiently for the person to come on the line.*

*"911 what's your emergency"?*

*"It's my mom, she's not breathing and there is blood coming out of her mouth."*

*"Ok, calm down," the dispatcher says.*

*I struggle to stay calm and belt out my address. The dispatcher instructs me on how to give my mom CPR. It seems like hours before the ambulance arrives but when they do, I'm thankful.*

*I watch in horror as they work on her. Finally they put her on a stretcher and push her out of the house. I follow on their heels. I ask if I can ride along and they let me.*

*All the way to the hospital I cry. My mom doesn't wake up the whole time we're in the ambulance. Once at the hospital, they take her stretcher out and push it down a hall.*

*Again I follow as fast as my little legs will take me. They pull her into a room and a nurse blocks my path.*

*"I have to go in there. That's my mom!" I scream.*

*"I'm sorry we can't let you in there. You have to wait out here. Someone will come get you when we're ready, ok?"*

*I listen to and obey the woman but I don't like it. I sit on a bench. I wait. I bite my nails and bounce my leg for what seems like an eternity.*

*I look at my phone several times. I don't even know who to call. It's not like we have any other family of anything. It was only my mom and me.*

*Us against the world we would say. The memory makes me sad and I begin to cry. Sobs rack my body and I finally lose control. A woman comes over and tries to comfort me.*

*I don't register who she is, I just hold onto her for dear life. After a while a man comes out with a mask hanging from his face. He pulls off his gloves and walks over to me. His face is pale and his expression stony.*

*"Hi, I'm Doctor Walker," he says.*

*"I'm Sky," I say. "Is my mom going to be ok?"*

*"Well, she has had surgery and we've done the best that we can for her. She doesn't have long," he says. "Is there someone we can call for you? Your dad?"*

*I crumble to the floor at his words. I cry and cry,* shaking my head no. I grab my head in my hands and scream this isn't happening over and over. Sometime later I am taken to my mother's room.

I gaze at all of the machines that are hooked up to her. There is a machine moving her chest up and down. There are all sorts of tubes in her mouth and nose.

*She looks like she's asleep. She looks like my Grandmother did when she was asleep in the box. All sorts of images fly through my head and I feel alone. My mother is gone and she's not coming back. Ever. I'm alone.*

*I walk over and grab her hand. I lay my head on her chest and cry until I can't cry anymore. I sense people coming in the room and I barely look up. I stare into the face of a man that looks familiar.*

*My father.*

## *Chapter 18*

Crying at the memory of my mother, I pull away from Sue. "I can't do this again," I say in a voice full of hurt.

Just when I'm about to leave, Bill comes out smiling.

"She's awake!" he exclaims in a happy tone.

We all head back into the room and sure enough, those big beautiful blue eyes have opened. I close my own eyes and thank God or whoever is responsible for bringing her back. Tears of joy stream down my face and I feel my sadness being replaced by happiness.

"Sky?" Casey says in a raspy voice. I walk to her bed slowly.

"Please tell me I'm not dreaming. Please tell me you're actually awake and talking to me."

"Yes, this is real and yes, I'm talking to you." She tries to smile but grimaces as pain washes over her.

I take her hand. "I am so happy that you're ok. I was so worried I had lost you."

I finally break down and fall into her arms, careful not to hurt her. She runs her uninjured hand through my hair to sooth me.

"It's ok," she says drowsily. "I'm ok and I'm here honey." She places a kiss in my hair. I look up at her and smile.

"I love you!" I blurt out.

My words startle her but she recovers and says, "I love you too."

We smile at each other stupidly and her parents come over. I pull back and Casey says, "I need to talk to you girlfriend, so don't leave."

I swallow the lump in my throat, shrug, and back away. I watch as her parents hug and talk to her. I take a seat in the corner and crash from all the emotions I've gone through today.

I shut my eyes and take a deep breath. I promise myself I will never hurt Casey again. As long as I have breath in my body,

I will try to be the best person I can be for myself as well as her.

A while later, I say goodbye to her parents. Casey and I are left in the room. I walk back to the bed and sit down.

"Hi," I say grabbing her hand.

"Hi," she says smiling at me. "So you told my parents that you are my girlfriend?"

"I'm sorry. I didn't know what else to say. I didn't want to raise any questions about why I was here," I say in a rushed voice.

"Did you mean it?"

"Huh?" I ask confused.

"Did you mean it - the girlfriend part," she repeats.

"Yes," I say in a confident tone. "If you'll have me, then yes, I am your girlfriend."

Casey blushes and says, "Yes."

I jump out of my seat and kiss her with all I have. I try to tell her with my kisses how much she means to me. I pour myself into her and take all that she has to give.

## *Chapter 19*

I visit her every day. The day she gets released finally approaches. "Casey, I was thinking that you should just come to my place so that I can look after you," I say logically.

She ponders my offer for a while. I become nervous and try to back pedal.

"I mean, I can help you out at your…your place," I stammer.

She smiles and finally has mercy on me. "Sure honey, that's a great idea. I was just enjoying you stammering."

I tap her shoulder jokingly and tell her how mean she is. Once at my house, I fuss and take extra care getting her in the apartment. I make her comfortable on the sofa and she finally yells at me to stop.

"You're so adorable when you're fussing she says."

I blush. "I just want you to be comfortable."

Casey stayed in the hospital long enough to get her cast off her leg but still has the cast on her arm. She still has some nasty cuts and bruising but other than that, she was very lucky. I take a seat beside her and ask her to tell me what happened.

"Well, I was driving to work in that bad storm we were having. The traffic lights had been struck by lightning. I slowed my car down so I could be extra careful and this huge truck came barreling down the street going way too fast. I didn't have time to move and it collided with my car. I was instantly knocked out. All I remember after that is waking up in the hospital."

I hug her to me. "That must have been very frightening but you're safe now."

She smiles. "What happened at the fair that day?

I take a deep breath and decide honesty is the best way to handle this. "Valerie is a friend of mine that I slept with on occasion. I blew her off when I started having feelings for you and I guess it upset her. Running into her at the fair caught us both off guard. I hadn't expected to see her. I know that I should have ended things and made them clear to her."

I take Casey's face into my hands and tell her, "I'm sorry. I truly never meant to hurt you. I never wanted any of this to happen. As long as I have breath in my body I will never ever hurt you again, I promise."

Her eyes well up with tears and we lean in at the same time. Taking her mouth with mine I kiss her lips and close my eyes. I run my tongue all over her lips, seeking permission to come inside.

She grants me permission and moans. Her mouth is warm and wet and I can go a lifetime just kissing her wonderful mouth.

We break the kiss breathing frantically. I rest my forehead against hers and breathe her scent in. Honey and flowers envelope my whole being. "I love you," I whisper.

"I love you too," she whispers back.

We curl up together on the sofa and drift off to sleep.

## *Chapter 20*

Time flies while we spend time healing and getting to know each other. I have learned that Casey's full name is Cassandra Love Taylor. I learned that she is thirty-four and like me is the only child.

She hates being called Cassandra and loves the color blue. Each day that passes, I continue to look forward to learning all there is to know about her.

Casey finally got her cast off and the bruises are fading. I'm excited at how well things are going between us. As we sit on the sofa and watch a movie, I turn and stare at Casey. Her brown hair is shines in the light.

Her eyes are focused and bright. I look at her and wonder how I ever survived without her in my life.

She senses me staring at her, turns, and looks at me. I pull her to me.

"I love you so much," I confess.

"I love you too," she says in a questioning voice.

I don't answer but pull her into a searing kiss. I suck on her bottom lip and pull it into my mouth. Casey moans.

We have refrained from any kind of activity while she was healing but I realize I can't wait any longer to have her. To make her mine.

I rise up and hold out my hand. She takes it. I lead her to the bedroom and sit her on the bed. I kneel and whisper, "I'm going to worship your body baby."

She blushes and places her hands on my shoulders. I ease her shirt over her head and soon after her bra follows. Kissing her lips, I then make my way down her neck. I continue to marvel at the beauty of this woman. She is like a blooming flower waiting to be plucked.

Her scent of flowers and honey fills my nostrils. Breathing her scent in deeply, I take her nipple in her mouth. Sucking gently, she moans.

"Oh yes she breathes."

I take the other nipple in my mouth and suck a little harder. Casey throws her head back and grabs my shoulders tighter.

I move downward with my mouth and continue to kiss and lick all over her body. I remember that she's ticklish so I lick around her belly button. She giggles.

I don't stay there very long. I continue my journey south. I have a destination in mind. I unbutton her jeans. I playfully pull the zipper down with my teeth and I hear her sharp intake of breath.

"You like that?" I ask.

"Yes," comes the soft reply. Her jeans and underwear come off without any trouble. I adore her nakedness.

"You're so beautiful."

"Thank you," she says shyly.

I lick her thighs. She spreads her legs. She lays back.

"Sit up. I want you to watch as I lick your pussy."

She moans. I lock eyes with her as I slide my tongue through her folds. Casey gasps and closes her eyes.

"Open your eyes," I say in a commanding voice.

She opens them and once again I stare into the blue heaven of her eyes. I lick her folds. I run my tongue from top to bottom. I take her lips in my mouth and suck.

"Oh God!" she moans.

I suck a little harder and add my fingers to the mix. I insert one, then two fingers into her wet pussy.

She gasps and grinds against my fingers. Her scent is a mix of flowers and something sweet. She tastes unbelievable. I could do this forever.

I pick up the pace. I pump my fingers in and out of her.

Faster.

Rougher.

Casey arches her back. I feel her body tense. I ready myself for her release. I don't stop.

"Oh fuck! I'm going to cum!" she screams.

"Let it go baby," I coax.

When she comes down from her orgasm I lay beside her. I kiss her mouth and we share her juices.

The moment is intense and erotic for us both. I stand up to shed my clothes and go in the drawer next to my bed. I pull out my strap-on.

"Is this is ok?"

"Ummm. I've never tried that before."

"We should try it together."

"Ok," she says after a moment.

I buckle the strap-on up and lubricate it. I notice that she is nervous, so I lie in between her legs and kiss her.

I get her calm and continue kissing her wonderful mouth. I place kisses on her neck and ready myself to enter her.

I hold the strap-on and place the head at her entrance. I gaze into her eyes. I push all the way in.

"Fuck," I say as the feelings take over my body.

Casey gasps loudly and grabs my back. She wraps her legs around me while I wait patiently for her to become accustomed to the feeling of me inside her.

She settles with her legs around me and I start to move. Pulling it all the way out and pushing back in again causes Casey to moan. She grabs a handful of my hair and pulls me closer to her.

"Damn you feel good baby," I say panting. "I don't know how long I will be able to last. My orgasm is building.

"Mine too," she breathes and moves more in sync with me.

We increase our speed. We become frantic. We search for our release. I push into her harder. And harder. We are both moaning.

"Cum with me now!" I shout.

"Yes!" she screams.

I thrust roughly inside her a few more times as we release together.

"Oh god yes! Yes! Yes! Yes!" Casey screams. "Oh Sky! God yes!"

Casey digs her nails in my back. I know that will leave marks but I don't even care or let it register. I continue to thrust inside her, feeling my release.

When we calm, another orgasm hits her body. Holding on to her, I ride out her release.

We part, panting and breathing hard.

"Jesus that was amazing," I say.

"I agree that was fantastic," Casey nods.

We smile at each other and she lies in my arms. I pull the covers over us. We fall asleep spent and satisfied.

## *Chapter 21*

I stand in front of the mirror, nervous. I
stare at myself. I look at the face of a
changed woman. I have changed in so many
ways, all for the better.

Casey is the best thing that could have
ever happened to me. She has had a major
impression on me.

Gone are the shadows that haunted me
day in and day out. Gone is the never
ending hurt I felt all the time. Gone is the
shadow of a person I once was. Gone is the

loneliness that wouldn't leave. Gone is the ice which had replaced my heart.

In its place is love. Love covers my being and makes me a new person. I no longer drink to feel numb but drink for fun. I no longer go through life searching and searching for a feeling, an emotion, and a life. I have one now.

I straighten my jacket and smooth out my shirt. I smile at my reflection. Today, on June the seventh, I am marrying the woman I'm in love with.

I say yes to Casey Taylor to be my wife, to have and to hold from this day forward, for better, for worse, for richer, for poorer, in sickness and in health, to love and to cherish, till death us do part.

I smile at the words forming in my head. I step outside and look up at the sky. There in the clouds and the great blue expanse are familiar faces staring back at me.

I smile and tears come into my eyes. My grandmother and mother stare at me, their eyes shining brightly. They smile at me.

The sun warms my skin and I continue to stare at the faces. My Grandmother blows me a kiss. My mother gives me a thumb up.

I hear them whisper they will always be with me no matter what path I choose. I allow tears to stream down my cheeks. They disappear into the sky.

I wipe my face and the door opens to the church. With one last glance back at the sky I stroll happily through the doors.

The end

# *About the Author*

Ivey Weaver is 32 years old from a small town in Florida called Deland. One of five children, she  has three brothers and a sister. Ivey started writing when she was 14 years old. Growing up, experiencing so many things, writing became her escape and her passion.

Ivey considers herself to be her own worst critic. Starting out writing poetry then short stories, Ivey found her voice in her words. While completing her degree in Psychology at the University of Phoenix, not sure what to do with her degree; she decided she wanted to follow her passion of writing and be a full time Author.

Ivey and her wife co-wrote and created *"Mrs & Mrs: A Journey from Will You to I Do"* and founded *"Lez'Luv Her"* an online store where their products promote equal love. Ivey currently lives in Massachusetts with her wife and step-son.

www.ingramcontent.com/pod-product-compliance
Lightning Source LLC
Chambersburg PA
CBHW070943190726
48292CB00004B/1310